FINAL WISHES

A Cautionary Tale
on Death,
Dignity
& Physician-
Assisted Suicide

Paul Chamberlain

InterVarsity Press
Downers Grove, Illinois

InterVarsity Press
P.O. Box 1400, Downers Grove, IL 60515
World Wide Web: www.ivpress.com
E-mail: mail@ivpress.com

InterVarsity Press® is the book-publishing division of InterVarsity Christian Fellowship/USA®,
a student movement active on campus at hundreds of universities, colleges and schools of
nursing in the United States of America, and a member movement of the International
Fellowship of Evangelical Students. For information about local and regional activities, write
Public Relations Dept., InterVarsity Christian Fellowship/USA, 6400 Schroeder Rd., P.O. Box
7895, Madison, WI 53707-7895.

All Scripture quotations, unless otherwise indicated, are taken from the Holy Bible, New
International Version®. NIV®. Copyright ©1973, 1978, 1984 by International Bible Society. Used
by permission of Zondervan Publishing House. All rights reserved.

Cover photograph: Peter Delory/Image Bank

ISBN 0-8308-2259-3

Printed in the United States of America ∞

Library of Congress Cataloging-in-Publication Data
Chamberlain, Paul, 1954-
    Final wishes : a cautionary tale on death, dignity & physician-assisted suicide / Paul
Chamberlain.
    p. cm.
    Includes bibliographical references.
    ISBN 0-8308-2259-3 (paper : alk. paper)
    1. Assisted suicide—United States—Case studies. 2. Terminally ill—United States—Case
studies. I. Title.
R726.C45 2000
174'.24—dc21
                                                                            99-086866

15 14 13 12 11 10 9 8 7 6 5 4 3 2 1
11 10 09 08 07 06 05 04 03 02 01 00

I dedicate this book to two people
without whom it may never have been written.

The first is Gail, my wife of twenty years.
Her constant support and encouragement—
in spite of my many professionally induced absences
and late suppers—
has enabled me to complete this project.

The second is Helen, my mother,
who at the time of publication still carries on
her thirty-year battle with multiple sclerosis.
Her indomitable courage through suffering
is a big part of what inspired me to examine the question
of physician-assisted suicide.
She and others like her are the heroes in this issue.

Acknowledgments

This book arose out of a series of public forums I participated in with two people. One forum was with Mr. Svend Robinson, a member of Canada's parliament. Six others were with Dr. Faye Girsh, the executive director of the Hemlock Society. The topic of the forums was the same as that of this book, and the research for these events formed the basis of this project. The arguments and questions put to me by both Mr. Robinson and Dr. Girsh helped me clarify precisely what is important to people on both sides of this question and thus have been invaluable for the writing of this book. I am indebted to both of them.

In addition, many friends and colleagues have helped this book see the light of day. My thanks go to John Penner, who once again provided the initial idea for the story line. His creativity was instrumental in launching this project. I also wish to thank my colleague Michael Horner, whose searching questions forced me to fine tune the views and arguments treated here. I am also grateful for my assistants, Heidi Meier and Michael Martens, who took part in the research for the book and also provided many helpful comments on both its arguments and story line. Victor Arneill, my adviser, read the completed manuscript and made many suggestions on all aspects of the work. Many of these suggestions have found their way into the story. Shane Beasley applied his graphic arts specialty to the cover of this book. His insightful suggestions have resulted in a number of improvements to it.

My greatest thanks, however, are reserved for my family, Gail, Tyler and James. I will never forget for their unswerving support and encouragement to me during the time I have given to this enterprise.

1

Ron tightened the seat belt and gripped the armrests as the plane began its descent. He tried not to think about the various reports of plane accidents he had seen on the news even this last week. He tried not to question himself about whether the pilots were ready for such a situation. He tried not to imagine what it would feel like to crash.

Suddenly the fuselage leaned hard to the right, and he felt the engines rev up as the plane momentarily lifted and then settled back again. Then, just as suddenly, the engines cut back as the plane dropped noticeably, causing his stomach to leap into his throat. The young girl sitting next to him searched frantically in the pouch in front of her for, he guessed, the little bag. Her face was ashen, and it was clear that she could not take much more of this. It would not be a soft landing; he was pretty sure of that.

Man, I hate that feeling, he mumbled to himself. *Total loss of control. My life is in someone else's hands and there's not a thing I can do about it.* He looked down and saw his knuckles—white from clutching the armrest in a viselike grip.

Personal control over one's own life: a strongly desired commodity

Without warning the plane jolted and lurched back as the wheels touched down and the reverse thrusters roared to life, pushing the passengers forward in their seats. Through the vast amounts of blowing snow, Ron saw the flashing lights of the snow-removal vehicles as they pushed their way up and down the runways.

He breathed a huge sigh of relief, then recovered his

luggage and headed to the terminal. As the adrenaline rush caused by the landing subsided, Ron's original anxiety returned. He thought of the loving kiss his wife had given him that morning and the harmonious relationship it represented, contrasted with the sad business that drew him away from her. Although he always looked forward to seeing Patrick, this tragic turn of fate in his friend's life was not the pleasant context he would have hoped for in his next visit.

Dr. Ron Grey was a second-generation doctor and had grown up observing his father's love for his work and patients. He also had come to appreciate the comfortable life his father had provided for his family compared with that of Ron's grandparents and other relatives. Vacations, trips, restaurant meals, newer cars and homes. He was determined to follow in his father's footsteps.

Ron and Patrick had aspired to be doctors in high school, and both had been accepted at the University of Toronto medical school. They had stayed together throughout, and though they had parted ways after that, they had remained in close contact. The intervening twenty-or-so years had been good for both of them, with Pat joining a practice in the Chicago area and Ron doing the same in Winnipeg. Their jobs were rewarding and their family lives were happy. Until three months ago.

Ron recalled the shocking news that had informed him that Patrick had been diagnosed with ALS, a fatal degenerative disease. The chill he had felt then remained with him even now. As disturbing as the initial phone call had been, it was the most recent one that had driven Ron's decision to make this trip. Patrick's words were indelibly imprinted on his mind: "You've got to help me," he had pleaded. "I don't want to go through all the pain and suffering that I know is coming. And I certainly don't want Jean and the kids to have to go through it either. But I won't be able to end it all myself, and you are the only one I can count on." When Ron only listened in stunned silence, Patrick had added the words, "Can't I? Right? I

The normal desire to avoid suffering

can count on you, can't I?" He had sounded depressed, almost pitiful. Nothing like the Patrick Ron had known. How in the world should he respond?

The very next day Ron had decided to book a flight so he could talk to Patrick in person and try to sort things out. At the last moment he had forced himself to pack a small medical kit containing, among other things, doses of morphine and potassium chloride and two syringes. The possibility that he might use the kit had sent another shudder through him.

From their past discussions Ron knew that Patrick approved, in principle, of physician-assisted suicide. But this was no longer a philosophical question. This was a friend asking for help. Ron was troubled by the whole situation. He too had always accepted some vague notion of a person's right to live or die, but had felt a nagging reluctance to become involved. He suddenly found himself thrust into the heart of an issue that he had no desire to engage at all.

The common tendency to avoid controversial issues

The taxi ride to Pat and Jean's offered some peace and quiet for Ron to rest. Not really seeing what he was doing, he paged through the *Newsweek* he had grabbed before boarding the plane. The cover story was about troop movements in the Middle East, but something near the bottom of the page caught his attention: "Illinois Senate to Decide Right to Die." *Coincidence?* Ron wondered. He flipped to the story and found out, to his surprise, that during the very week of his visit with Pat, the Illinois senate was holding hearings on physician-assisted suicide. He noted the time and location and started to think about how he might get access to those hearings. He wondered if Pat's decision had anything to do with them.

2

The large and well-kept houses of Lake Forest streamed past as the taxi headed down Westleigh Road. Ron had once envied Pat's good fortune, but that had all changed. The taxi turned into the long, winding driveway. A new engraved sign at the entrance read, "The Metcalfes, Pat and Jean." As usual the grounds were well kept, all three acres of them, but they showed the effects of a harsh winter. The house was a large, Tudor-style mansion, renovated up and down. Ron knew that Pat and Jean had pampered and coddled it. New windows. New doors. A security system. Even a weight room, Ron had been told. The view of the nearby lake from the top floor of the home was captivating.

As the taxi pulled up to the house, Ron noticed an attractive woman wearing a heavy parka with the hood resting neatly on her back, revealing fashionably trimmed, dark brown hair. She seemed to be about to take two black Labradors for a walk, and she was only moderately surprised at the taxi's arrival. Ron nervously stepped out. All he could manage was a bittersweet smile. He couldn't help but notice the effects of the stress that the past few weeks had put on her.

"Jean . . ." Ron mumbled as he put his arm around her, trying to keep a brave face as tears welled up in his friend's wife's eyes.

"Thanks so much for coming, Ron. Pat is really looking forward to seeing you."

Ron was pale, unsure of anything significant to say at

this moment. "I just wish the situation were different. How are you holding up?"

"I need to be strong for Pat," she said, "but we've never had to go through anything like this before."

Ron fumbled with his wallet as the taxi driver's patience began to wane. This was going to be more difficult than he had anticipated.

"Everything has changed now," Jean continued. "Our life. Our plans. Even our relationship. Do you know what it's like being married to someone who wants to die?"

Ron shook his head silently. He hadn't a clue.

The devastating changes brought by serious illness

"I know he won't be here much longer, and I often find myself wondering what he'll be like in a month, two months or half a year if he's still here."

Ron felt powerless to help. *Feels like the plane landing,* he thought.

"He's waiting for you. We better go." Jean opened the door to let Ron and his luggage in, then disappeared into the house. Ron heard some noise around the corner, and then a somewhat familiar—if off-balance and shuffling—figure moved toward him. It was Pat. Ron was surprised at the metamorphosis that his friend had undergone since he had last seen him. Although the familiar beard was still well trimmed, Pat's face seemed longer, more haggard. The shortness of his stature seemed emphasized by an invisible weight on his shoulders. There was a slight slur in his speech when he greeted Ron.

"I knew you'd come," he said.

Ron grabbed him and they embraced each other, their tears mingling. "It's so good to be here," he said, realizing he had mixed feelings about his words.

"Why don't I show you your room so you can get settled, then we'll talk."

"Sounds great." Ron's words felt empty, despite the empathy in his heart. Pat led Ron into the house and showed him to a guest room on the upper level. It was large and well equipped, containing a television, a radio, a desk and chair, and a view of the lake. Ron shut the door and set down his luggage. The medical kit was safely packed inside. Immediately he picked up the phone and dialed his home.

"Hello?" the voice on the other end sounded restrained and uncertain.

"Hi, Love." Ron yearned for his wife. He needed her embrace.

"You sound like you need a hug. How is everything? How are Pat and Jean?"

"I don't know how to answer that. It's tough, Judy. It's like nothing else I can imagine."

"Any insights as to how you are going to handle this?"

"That's what makes it even tougher. I have no idea. I just got here and I haven't talked with either of them about it yet. It would be one thing to be asked to give comfort or encouragement to them, but to be asked to help him die . . ."

"I know." She was almost whispering. "You're his friend and you're a doctor. That's why you're there."

"I'd better go. Jean has coffee and a snack waiting. I love you, Judy."

"I love you too, Ron. Take care of yourself, and please call back sooner. OK?"

"Yes, Dear," Ron groaned, like he always did when he teased his wife.

"Hey!"

"Sorry, Sweetheart. I'll call you soon." Ron hung up the phone and followed the smell of coffee down the stairs. Jean had put out deli meat and fresh-baked buns along with some pastry and a pot of the richest coffee Ron had drunk in a while.

"In the den, Ron!" Pat called out. He was sitting in a leather recliner with a plate of food on the side table, a cup of coffee in his hand and a warmer on his legs. The dogs were wrestling on the floor, and Ron could not avoid the contrast between their vitality and Pat's deterioration.

The north and west walls of the den were lined with book-laden oak shelves. The south wall was fitted with a comfortable, beige love seat, which was next to Pat's chair and the dogs. Ron sat down in the love seat. If so many thoughts were not troubling him, he might have easily dozed off.

Jean joined them a few moments later and broke the silence. She nervously asked about Judy, the children, Ron's practice, their home—all the usual small-talk. Ron answered with whatever enthusiasm he could muster and then politely returned the questions. Judy reported that Pat's practice was winding down. His last day was to be at the end of the month, three weeks away, and he was only going in four hours each day now.

Jean commented that Pat's disease seemed to be progressing quickly although no one really knew for certain. The limp had just started three days earlier and already caused him greater unsteadiness. Sometimes the deterioration goes fast and sometimes it goes slow, his neurologist had told them. He might need a wheelchair soon. No one could say for sure. Ron felt sick to his stomach as he pondered the devastation this ugly disease was about to bring upon his friend.

After quietly sipping coffee for a minute or so, Pat looked at Jean awkwardly, then turned to Ron. "There's something else we need to tell you," he said.

What now? Ron wondered.

"It's about the media."

"The media?" Ron looked confused.

"Yes. ATN to be exact."

"What does ATN have to do with you?" Ron asked, fearing that Pat was about to tell him something big. ATN was one of the nation's major networks, with satellite stations throughout the country. Every day millions of viewers tuned in to get their news and entertainment from this impressive media giant.

"Nothing, until last week," Jean replied. "Somehow they got wind of Pat's illness, and two reporters stopped by last Friday."

"They called themselves investigative journalists," Pat added.

"And asked you what?" Ron was growing suspicious.

There was another awkward pause. "They want to do a story on us," Pat finally replied nervously, as if he knew his long-time friend would not be happy to hear this.

"A story?" Ron exclaimed, bolting forward to the edge of his chair.

Pat was startled. "They want to follow the progression of my illness through a series of interviews."

"A series?" Ron was on the edge of the love seat, almost rising to his feet.

"They think it could have educational value for the country," Pat replied.

Jean leaned forward. "The man explained that it would give people insight into ALS and how it affects a person who has it and the person's family. He said it could have great benefit for their viewers all around the country."

"Not to mention what it could do for their own ratings," Ron replied cynically. "Vultures," he muttered under his breath, loud enough so that Pat and Jean could hear. "Parasites."

"So you don't like the idea?"

"That's very perceptive, Pat. The idea stinks! What business have these people got coming in here, pressuring you like this? They're making you feel like if you don't do this, you're denying all this benefit to the world, like you have some obligation here. You don't! Do these people have no limits at all? No decency, no sensitivity to a person's need for privacy, especially when they are dealing with something like ALS? What kind of people are these who would take advantage of a person when he's down so they can boost their own ratings?"

Pat looked over at Jean and sucked in a large breath, then slowly exhaled. They had wondered how Ron might respond, but they weren't prepared for anything this intense.

Ron spoke again. "You're not going to do it, are you?"

There was a long, uncomfortable silence.

"C'mon, Pat!" Ron lectured and begged at the same time.

"They're coming tomorrow," Pat replied quietly but firmly.

Ron was dumbfounded. He looked at the floor and whispered, "Tomorrow." After a few seconds of silence he looked up. "You don't have to do this! Especially not tomorrow! Why such a rush?"

"We had to make a decision . . . quickly," Pat said. "We're not dealing with a lot of time here."

Ron slumped back on the love seat, silently shaking his head. "I don't believe this," he whispered. "You can still call it off," he said. "I'll call the vultures myself if you want."

"I don't *want* to call it off," Pat said. "We've decided the country could use some education about this disease, and the people at ATN say they can make it happen."

Ron bolted upright again. "You don't for a moment believe they're doing this out of some noble ambition to disseminate truth, do you? It's ratings, ratings, ratings! That's all these people care about. They live by ratings. They monitor them all the time. If your story wasn't good for the ratings, they wouldn't do it!"

"Whoa! Whoa!" Pat raised his hand. "I don't know what their motives are, but I do know the country could use some education on this disease and on why a person who has it might want to choose physician-assisted suicide."

Ron froze. "You've told them that too?"

"Told them what?"

"That you want a physician-assisted suicide?"

"I didn't have to. They knew it already. They seemed to know a lot of things by the time they arrived at the house. These people have got ears everywhere."

It suddenly hit Ron like a ton of bricks. That was why the media were taking such an interest in Pat and Jean.

With the debate in the Illinois state senate on physician-assisted suicide just days away, the entire country was turning its attention to this issue. And here was a prominent local physician, struck down with ALS and, at this very moment, making it clear that he wanted the legislature to legalize the practice so he could receive the service. Could there be a better story? It had controversy. It was about one man pitted against the system, and it involved real people, not mere numbers, facts, or arguments.

Ron turned to Jean. "I hope you realize that a good portion of this will fall to you," he said. "It's only a matter of time before Pat becomes incommunicative."

"I know," Jean whispered.

Turning back to Pat, Ron said, "Let me guess." His words dripped with cynicism. "They want to do a lot of their interviewing in the next week or so, *before* the vote is taken in the senate?"

Pat looked at Jean and chuckled knowingly. "Yes. They want one tomorrow and another on Saturday."

"Two interviews in two days."

"They want to ask a lot of questions at the beginning, while I still have strength to do this," Pat smiled.

"Sure," Ron smiled back. "It looks like we've got our work cut out for us."

"They promised it won't be hard," Jean interjected, helpfully. "No preparation. Just tell our story."

3

The ATN vans arrived the next morning at precisely ten o'clock, as promised, and in thirty minutes the crew turned Pat and Jean's dining room into a recording studio. Plants and pictures were rearranged. Microphones, lights and cameras were set up. A thousand cords crisscrossed on the floor. "Don't worry," they assured Pat and Jean. "We'll put it all back in order before we leave. You'll never know we were here."

"Dream on," Ron muttered under his breath, from a distance.

Meanwhile another camera operator was walking outside, taking shots of the property—the well-kept yard and the beautifully restored home. These would add to the personal touch they wanted to create with this story.

A host of technical people took up their positions in the room as Jean and Pat sat down on one side of the dining room table. Miniature lapel microphones were clipped onto them, and powerful lights glared down, brightening and warming the room considerably. The two black Labradors were nestled comfortably on the floor next to Pat, who occasionally leaned over to stroke them.

On the other side of the table were two reporters. One was a woman in her early forties. She was short and pretty, with medium-length brown hair. Julia Benthall was not only highly articulate, but she also had a smile so warm and sincere that even Ron's resistance to the interview was softened considerably. Of course, he still would have preferred that they not be there.

The other reporter was a tall man in his late fifties, obviously a highly experienced journalist. His name was Fritz Mahoney. His short, curly hair was perfectly trimmed, and he wore a navy two-piece suit, a conservative tie and a light-colored shirt. ATN had obviously sent two of its more experienced reporters out for this assignment.

Ron made himself scarce, watching the interview from an inconspicuous corner of the room, unseen by the cameras and unnoticed by most everyone else. Pat had introduced him earlier as simply Ron, a friend who was visiting for a few days. Pat, Jean and Ron had agreed that it was imperative for Ron to remain unknown to these reporters. In the event that the law in favor of physician-assisted suicide did not pass, Pat would need a physician whose identity had not been broadcast around the country on the national networks—not to mention how uneasy Ron felt about the idea of becoming known nationally as the physician who helped a colleague die.

Julia Benthall led off and spoke directly to Pat. "Dr. Metcalfe, would you please introduce yourself and your wife?"

Pat identified himself and gave a brief summary of his career as a physician and his role as a husband and father. Then placing his arm around Jean's shoulders, he said, "This is my wife of twenty-one years, Jean. She is standing by me through this, and I love her for it." Jean breathed deeply and held her composure.

"You have ALS, is that correct?" Julia proceeded.

"Yes."

"What do those letters stand for?"

Explaining ALS "Amyotrophic lateral sclerosis," Pat replied. "My illness is also referred to as Lou Gehrig's disease."

"Could you please tell us about this illness? What is it? What does it do to a person who contracts it?"

Pat spoke slowly and precisely. "ALS is a progressive, fatal neuromuscular disease."

Julia smiled sincerely and nodded. "For the benefit of

us lay people, what does that mean?"

"It means that this disease destroys nerves that control all voluntary muscles. When they aren't being used, the muscles die. In most cases, over a period of two to five years, the body of someone who has this illness becomes completely debilitated even though the mind remains clear."

"Debilitated?"

"Yes. Paralyzed."

Julia turned toward Jean. "Mrs. Metcalfe," she asked softly, "Is there anything you would like to add about your husband's illness?"

Jean leaned forward, folding her hands on the table. "As Pat said, this disease is also fatal. My husband will eventually die from his illness. On average, once diagnosed, a person lives two to five years, although some live decades." Julia shook her head slowly as Jean continued. "This is not a disease one fights alone. It is a family diagnosis. It's going to affect all of us in the family."

"Is there anything comforting or encouraging that you can tell us about ALS?"

"Comforting? Encouraging?" Jean looked directly into the reporter's eyes. Julia shifted uncomfortably in her chair. Then Jean responded with a statement she had heard from Ron just the night before. "This disease is one of nature's cruelest jokes," she said. "The only thing that could be called comforting, as you say, is that it is not hereditary. You don't get it from your parents, nor do you pass it on to your children. Some may derive comfort from that."

Sensing that his colleague was struggling, Fritz Mahoney quickly picked up the ball and turned to Jean. "How would you describe the life you and your husband have had together over the past twenty-one years?" he asked.

"Active and happy," she responded in an instant. "Pat has worked hard, up to eighty hours a week at times, but we have also played hard. We've gone on drives and mini-vacations, and we've always enjoyed a variety of both summer and winter sports."

Fritz Mahoney looked at Patrick. "How did you know you had ALS?"

Initial indicators of ALS "I didn't . . . at first," Pat replied. "There were little signs that something wasn't right, but I thought nothing of them."

"Signs?"

"Yes. I had water-skied for thirty years," Pat said, "and suddenly one day I couldn't hang on to the rope or get out of the water. I just thought I must be out of shape. Then I had trouble lifting my arms for things like washing the car or putting on a tie."

Jean leaned forward and spoke. "Then one day I noticed he was getting narrow across the shoulders."

Pat looked directly at Jean. "When she told me that, it scared me," he said. "Because I knew that was typical of the muscle atrophy caused by ALS."

Ron sat across the room, nodding, knowing Pat was right.

"Then it was my balance," Pat continued, sounding discouraged. "It still is. I took a fall down those steps." He waved toward the flight of stairs going up to Ron's room. "And we both knew we couldn't ignore the symptoms any longer."

Ron flinched. He had heard none of this before. Pat began to weep quietly, and Jean slipped her arm around his shoulders.

"Could we take a break here?" she cut in, rather forcefully.

"Of course," Julia replied. She signaled a man standing directly behind Ron, obviously the chief production person, who in turn sliced his fingers across his throat. Instantly the cameras and lights were turned off. Jean continued to hold Pat, speaking softly to him. Ron eased out a side door to get some air.

In a few moments everyone was back. Fritz had promised that this initial interview would not be a long one. "Just introductions and background," he had said. "It'll give us all a feel for how it works, and we'll get to know each other."

Fritz resumed the questioning. "When did you learn that it was ALS?" he asked them.

"The neurologist gave us the news at his office six weeks ago," Jean said, speaking for both of them.

Fritz looked as if he was in pain. "How do you respond to news like that?" he asked, lifting both hands.

Jean paused, her eyes looking distant. "At first it was just disbelief," she said. "This couldn't be happening—not to us. We had talked about the possibilities, and ALS was the one disease we didn't want."

Fritz and Julia shook their heads solemnly, in unison. "What did you do?" Fritz asked.

"We went out to the parking lot, and plopped down in the car and looked at the world," Jean replied. "It was a different place from that moment on, let me tell you. Then we drove. Driving has always been our way of working issues out or just spending time together. We drove to Milwaukee, then over to Madison where we took a motel room." ^{Dealing with ALS}

"It was actually a very precious time," Pat cut in. "We talked, we cried, we shouted, and at times we said nothing. We also made some crucial decisions about selling my practice, cutting back my working hours immediately, and planning for the day I would quit altogether."

Julia spoke again, shaking her head with a sincerity Ron had never before witnessed in a reporter. "That kind of grief," she said. "How have you handled it? I can only imagine how deep it must be."

Jean was dabbing her eyes. "I've never experienced grief like this before," she said. "For a while I couldn't even read a book or watch television. There's this huge dark cloud hanging over everything I do. Sometimes I'm overwhelmed by the enormity of it. We're trying to deal with the challenges on a day-to-day basis. ^{(a) Unimaginable grief and loss}

"The hardest thing is having to watch Pat give up more and more of the things he loves. Last week I was mowing the lawn, crying my eyes out, and I looked up and saw him watching me do the thing he used to love to do. I can't explain that kind of pain."

Julia looked down solemnly, knowing she couldn't understand it, let alone explain it.

"We try not to dwell on the ALS and where it's all headed," Pat said. "I haven't got strength for that. But sometimes it's hard not to dwell on it."

"Why is that?" Fritz asked.

Pat chuckled softly. "Last week I watched a television documentary about a woman in the final stages of ALS. I cried for an hour after seeing that."

Ron sat and listened, silently grieving for his two close friends. It struck him that here, in a room full of reporters, cameras and burning lights, he was getting an education on this disease that no medical textbook had ever given him.

(b) New Priorities Patrick's eyes lit up only when Fritz asked about their children. "They're what I live for now," he said, "and Jean, of course. I'm so proud of them." He proceeded to tell ATN what each was doing and where they were working. He even had a grandchild now "I guess I'm one of the lucky ones," he said. "I made it to fifty; I've got a wife, three kids and a grandchild; and I love my work."

As Ron listened, he noticed that Pat did not include in that list anything about his home, the beautiful acreage purchased eleven years ago or the considerable wealth he had managed to accumulate through a well-paying job, long hours and a few timely investments. It was his kids, his wife, his grandchild and his patients. These were what caused his eyes to light up.

The first interview ended forty-five minutes after it had begun, and it was clearly long enough for both Pat and Jean. The remainder of the morning was spent rearranging the furniture after the interview.

They said goodbye to the reporters and agreed that they would do it all again tomorrow. As the vans drove down the winding driveway toward Westleigh Road and back to Chicago, Patrick turned to Ron. "I'm glad you're here. Thanks. I don't suppose this is much fun for you either."

Ron studied the driveway at his feet, unable to look Patrick in the eyes.

4

—————

S aturday's interview started later, at two o'clock, with the crew arriving at a quarter after one for setup. They went to work, efficiently rearranging the room again, although with a few differences from the way it had been done the day before. This was to make it subconsciously obvious to viewers that the interviews were individual and were taking place at different times, Fritz said. People needed to know that with each interview Dr. Metcalfe's illness had progressed a little farther.

Great, Ron thought. The country gets to witness the demise of a man stricken with ALS. They get to watch week by week, in living color, as the ravages of ALS are poured out on this man, his friend. "Lowlifes," he muttered from the top of the stairs as he watched the crew's work.

Pat and Jean were again fitted with nearly invisible lapel microphones as they took their places at the table. Pat sipped from a cup of coffee as he waited for the interview to begin. Fritz Mahoney and Julia Benthall were talking quietly in one corner of the room but stopped immediately when they noticed Pat and Jean sitting at the table. The two black Labradors took up their places on the floor beside Pat and began to doze.

Ron eased down the stairs and across the room and seated himself in a recliner as the interview began. No one noticed or paid any attention to the visitor. They were all too busy going about the business of conducting an important interview.

Fritz led off, smiling warmly. "How do you feel today, Doctor?"

"I feel good," Pat replied with a smile. "In fact, I feel lucky!"

"Lucky?" Fritz sounded surprised.

"Yes. After our first interview I went for a drive and took in some of the nicest scenery in the country . . . and I did it with a good friend. When was the last time you took a good friend and went out to enjoy the beauty of nature?" he asked Fritz.

This amused Fritz and he smiled. "I admit it's been a while."

"Well let me remind you," Pat continued, sounding like he was prescribing a regimen for one of his patients to follow, "that life is too short to put experiences like this off. Most of us put things like this off far more than we should."

"That's true," Fritz replied, nodding as he realized how significant these words would be for a person in Patrick Metcalfe's shoes. Then, looking intently at Patrick, he asked, "Speaking of the shortness of life, isn't it true, Dr. Metcalfe, that you've actually made a decision to shorten the length of your own life?"

The decision to end one's life

"Yes, it is," Pat replied without hesitation.

"Could you tell us about that decision?"

Pat thought a minute while the cameras rolled, then spoke with careful precision. "I have decided to end my life, with the assistance of a physician, at some point in the future, when I choose to," he answered.

"In other words," Fritz said, "You've chosen to die through a physician-assisted suicide?"

"Yes."

Then it was Julia Benthall's turn. She leaned forward with a worried look. "But surely, Dr. Metcalfe, you must be aware that this is not legal. You must know that if you go through with this, both you and the physician who assists you would be violating the law. Are you prepared to do that?"

Patrick knew this question would be coming and had thought about his answer. "I hope I don't have to make that decision," he said, avoiding the question. "I'm hoping it won't be illegal for long."

"You're referring to the upcoming debate and vote in the state senate on physician-assisted suicide."

"Yes," Pat agreed. "If the senate legalizes this practice, then I, and others like me, won't be put in the position of having to break the law."

"Do you have a physician in mind to assist you?" Ron bolted upright and froze.

"Yes."

"Are you willing to give us this physician's name?" Ron's pulse jumped and he could feel blood rushing to his head.

"No," Pat replied.

"Why not?"

"It should be obvious why not. You just pointed out that this practice is illegal at the moment. This physician is taking a great risk for me, and the least I can do is protect this person's privacy." Ron smiled inwardly.

Julia pressed farther, obviously wanting to gain whatever information Pat was willing to give. "Is this physician male or female?"

"Why should that matter?"

Julia nodded silently, looking as if she had been rebuked.

"Is this physician a friend of yours?" she continued.

"Of course. I have hundreds of friends in the medical profession all around this country and beyond. You and I both know that if I tell you who this physician is you'll have satellite trucks and reporters in the physician's driveway in twenty-four hours."

When she finally realized it would be futile to try to get anything more about the identity of this mystery physician out of Pat, Julia moved on to other questions. *We have other ways,* she told herself.

"You sound like you've made up your mind to go through with this. Are you really convinced it's the right thing to do?"

The *moral* question: Is physician-assisted suicide (PAS) *right?*

"I know what I've decided to do, and what I believe the senate should do, yes."

"Why, in your opinion," Julia Benthall asked, "should the senate vote to legalize physician-assisted suicide?"

Pat paused, leaning over to stroke one of the Labradors.

"Beautiful dogs," commented Julia, allowing him time to answer her question.

"They're a man's best friends," Pat replied, "and we treat them better than we treat each other."

Julia was taken aback, unsure of whether she should pursue the matter. She did not want to use up precious minutes on something irrelevant to the issue at hand but decided that since Pat had raised it, one or two questions wouldn't hurt. "How's that?" she asked.

First argument for PAS: If PAS is illegal, aren't we treating animals more "humanely" than we treat humans?

"Think about it," Pat replied. "If I were an animal like this one right here and developed a debilitating disease or serious pain or suffering, they would put me out of my misery. They would end my life. They wouldn't let an animal go on suffering. That would be considered inhumane—uncompassionate."[1]

Julia nodded, now realizing there was some relevance here.

"But here I am, and others like me. I'll be suffering more each day. I'll have some pain, although not as much as some people. I'll lose my independence and probably my dignity as well. And yet when I ask to die to end *my* suffering, the answer is no . . . so far. Why can't people like me be treated at least as well as animals are treated?"

"I have to admit, you make it sound pretty reasonable."

The *critical* question: Can we justify refusal to help a suffering person die?

Patrick set his coffee cup down and leaned forward, looking intently at both reporters. "The way I see it," he said, "the question we in this society need to be asking is what rational reason there could be for insisting that a person continue to endure pain, suffering and indignity when that person would prefer to die."

"Whew!" Julia exclaimed. "I have never had the question put to me in that way."

"And I don't get it," Pat continued.

"Get what?"

"Why the answer isn't obvious. I want to die at the time of my choosing. I don't want to suffer, and if I were an animal, I'd be allowed to die. It would be inhumane to force me to suffer." Then he laughed. "Notice that word: *inhumane.* Somehow it's OK to treat humans inhumanely but not animals. Go figure."

It was obvious that both Julia Benthall and Fritz Mahoney found this fascinating. Fritz leaned forward, setting aside his prepared questions. This line of questioning was much more interesting than the one he had planned. "What are the laws on this at present?" he asked. "How exactly are we responding to people like yourself who ask to die? Is it a flat-out no?"

Patrick laughed and rolled his eyes, then looked at the ceiling. "That's the absurd part!" He threw both hands up in the air. "It's not no, and it's not yes. It's a little bit of both, and it does nothing for people like me, let me tell you."

"Help me out here a little, Dr. Metcalfe," Fritz said. "I'm afraid you lost me with that one."

"You've heard about the woman who had a neurological disease, paralyzed from the neck down," Pat said. "Jody D., they nicknamed her."

Fritz nodded.

"After a couple of years on the respirator she wanted to die. She had nothing to live for anymore, the news said. Everything that gave her pleasure was gone. So do you remember what they did?"

"Yes, I remember." Fritz said. "They shut off the respirator."

"That's right, and they did it with the help of a doctor. You can't have just anyone walk over and flip the switch. It must be done skillfully or the patient will choke to death. Her physician administered morphine, rendering her unconscious, and then took her off the respirator."

"So what's the problem?" Fritz asked.

"There isn't one so far. But change the situation just a

little. Suppose Jody D. was suffering from a disease, like mine for instance, where there was no respirator keeping her alive."

"Yes?"

"*Now* suppose she wanted to die. Remember, there is no treatment her doctor could withhold or withdraw. No switch to flip. The only switch would be a lethal dose of morphine or some other lethal injection to end her life painlessly. Would they give it to her? No way. She'd just have to suffer."

"Yes, the law sees these two cases as different, doesn't it?"

Second argument for PAS: There is no moral difference in similar circumstances between *killing* and *letting die.*

"And that's absurd, in my opinion," Pat replied, forcefully. "Both these people want to die, and both need a doctor's help, but because one happens to be lucky enough to have a respirator that can be turned off, she gets the help. The other one does not."

Julia Benthall leaned forward with a pained expression on her face. "But Dr. Metcalfe, in one case the doctor was merely *letting* the patient die by removing the respirator. In the other, the doctor would be *killing* the patient with a lethal injection. That sounds like an important difference to me."[2]

"You call it *killing* the patient," Pat replied. "I call it *helping the patient die.*"

"But it's still a lethal injection," Julia persisted.

"Of course it is. I just don't happen to see any meaningful difference between letting the patient die and helping or killing, as you say, in circumstances like this. If you ask me, it's a bunch of meaningless philosophical hair splitting. It's hypocrisy."

The ceiling fan rotated slowly above them. A few seconds passed before anyone said anything, seconds that would surely be edited out later. Then Julia turned to Jean. "Mrs. Metcalfe, how does it feel to have a husband who has decided to end his own life in this way, through a physician-assisted suicide, due to his illness? Are there any words that could describe your feelings?"

This was a hard question, but it was one Jean had

guessed would be coming and she had rehearsed her answer. Leaning forward and looking intently at Julia, she replied, "No words could ever describe my feelings as I watch my husband plan to end his own life. I simply can't communicate my feelings to you. There is grief, anger and indescribable disappointment. There is also the frustration of having unanswered questions."

"Such as?"

"Why Patrick? What has he ever done but serve his patients and be the best husband and father any family could hope for?"

Julia nodded warmly. "What do you think about physician-assisted suicide? Surely from where you sit you must have an opinion on this issue?"

Jean had prepared for this question as well. "I'm not a politician or lawyer," she replied. But I am a physician's wife, and I think most of us are ignoring the cause of this whole debate."

"The cause?"

"That's right."

"And what, in your view, is the cause?"

"The powers of modern medicine," she answered immediately.

"You're blaming the medical profession for this? How is that?"

"I'm not sure *blame* is the right word, but think about it. Today we live better and longer than ever. We die less tragically. Our children don't die as often. Infant mortality is low in developed countries like ours and we don't die of infectious diseases like we used to."

"So far I don't see the problem," Julia smiled.

"Well, the downside is that when we do die, it is often of a chronic disease that can bring a long and agonizing death. Diseases like ALS, multiple sclerosis, cancer, emphysema, congestive heart failure, stroke and AIDS. The process of death can go on and on, and can involve a lot of pain and suffering."

Julia leaned forward, motioning and searching for the

New medical technology: a driving force behind euthanasia requests right words. "And this causes people to look for . . . ?" Her voice trailed off.

"It causes people to look for a way to avoid that long, drawn-out suffering—or even the possibility of it," Jean said. "And when you combine that with the fact that people today want choices, that they want to participate in their own medical care more than ever before, you can see why this debate has arisen."

Pat had been listening and nodding in agreement. "She's on to something," he cut in. "And there's another point you should know."

"Which is?"

"That I could do this anyway with or without anyone's help."

"You mean commit suicide?" Julia clarified.

"Yes. I could take a gun and blow my head off. It would all be perfectly legal and it happens all the time. Terminally ill people do it, the elderly do it, and a gun is their weapon of choice."

Then Fritz spoke again. "But of course you are seeking a physician's assistance because the gun is not your preferred method?" He waited a moment for Patrick to answer.

"No one," Patrick finally began, and then continued more loudly, "no one should have to die that way, to make the final passage from life to death in such a violent and bloody way! And what is more," he raised his voice passionately, "no one should ever have to find Grandpa in the basement with his brains blown out."

Julia Benthall flinched. "Yes, that would be tragic," Mahoney murmured, half to himself.

What some suffering people desire: (1) a gentle and peaceful death, (2) control over death

"Yes it would," Pat said. People should, if they wish, be able to die a gentle, peaceful, quick, certain and humane death, surrounded by their loved ones, spiritual advisors and doctors. They should be made to feel like they have control over what happens at the end of life."

There was that word again. *Control.* A highly desired commodity, that was obvious. As Ron took in the interview, he felt like he had been hit with a ton of bricks. Was

Patrick right? If so, then maybe he had a duty to help him die. What an overwhelming thought. His greatest hope at the moment was that he would find help to sort this out in the days ahead.

***

The first two interviews were over and Fritz and Julia had pronounced them a roaring success. *This, of course, means that they will do wonders for the network's ratings and the commentators' own personal careers,* Ron thought as he overheard Fritz raving to Pat and Jean.

Segments of the interviews ran on the national news that evening as part of a larger story on physician-assisted suicide and the upcoming debate and vote in the Illinois state senate.

Short clips of Patrick describing ALS and his initial signs of it were included along with his assertion that we treat suffering animals better than we treat suffering humans. The cameras panned across the two black Labradors as he spoke. The announcer reported Pat's intention to seek a physician-assisted suicide and his sincere desire that the senate would make the service legal so that he would not be faced with the decision of whether to break the law.

Brief mention was made of the mystery physician, whose identity thus far remained a secret known only to Dr. Metcalfe and a few close friends.

***

Ron watched the news on the television in his guest room. When it was over, he shut it off, settled in the chair beside the phone and immediately began punching in his home phone number. It had been two days since he had talked with Judy, and he missed her.

"Ron!" she burst out, excitedly. "How are you?"

"I'm OK, I think."

"You think? What's been happening?"

"You wouldn't believe it if I told you. I wouldn't believe

it myself if I weren't here witnessing it all."

"What? Tell me! How are Pat and Jean?"

"They're full of surprises; that's how they are."

"What surprises?"

"The media, for one."

"The media?" Judy sounded flabbergasted.

"Yep. ATN to be exact."

She listened in amazement as Ron gave her a running commentary on the events of the past two days. He left nothing out. He told her about Pat and Jean's decision to do the interviews, the questions they were asked, his talks with Pat and his own new role as the mystery physician. She listened with nervous excitement and tried valiantly to be the encouraging wife. Finally she exhaled deeply and said, "So now you've got another challenge—to keep yourself secret. You're a hot commodity. I always knew you were." She laughed hard at her own comment.

Ron had trouble seeing the humor in it but was glad to have something to laugh about.

Then she turned serious. "What if they find out who you are?"

Ron wanted to assure her they wouldn't, but he knew that neither he nor anyone else could give such an assurance. The media knew how to dig up information like this. It was their job and they were good at it. What's more, he had let out word to a few people himself before he knew anything about the media.

After a few comments about the girls Ron said goodbye and fell into bed.

5

Ron needed a new perspective and more information. Pat had hooked him up with some friends in politics to see if Ron could get a seat at the state senate hearing. He had learned that the hearings were open to the public and that if he was early enough he would have no problem. However, Ron had also discovered that he could possibly make the tail end of a public conference on euthanasia that was being held in a large hotel in Springfield, the state capital. Apparently it had been planned as a preparatory information meeting for politicians, academics and concerned citizens to attend prior to the state hearings. It was a great opportunity, but Ron wasn't sure how much he could catch at such a late time.

Jean had graciously let Ron take her car, and he made it to the conference center in good time. Walking through the large glass doors into the lobby, he immediately found himself in the conference area. For a few minutes he stood around with coffee in hand, purchased from the cappuccino bar in the corner of the outer lobby, and observed the commotion. The place was abuzz with activity as men and women carrying attaché cases, file folders, legal pads and books came and went. A multitude of discussions filled the big room.

Some of the men wore business suits and wing tip shoes. Others wore denim jackets and hiking boots. Some were clean-cut and closely shaven; others wore beards and had hair reaching to their shoulder blades. The women's attire likewise ranged from business suits to well-worn jeans and T-shirts and everything in between. Some people were laughing; others were incredibly somber. *How can they all be discussing the same issues?* he wondered.

He strained to overhear some of the conversations as he walked through the room trying to appear nonchalant. He heard words and phrases like vulnerability, the slippery slope, gentle and peaceful death, dignity, misdiagnosis, the Netherlands, Jack Kevorkian, personal autonomy, human equality and a host of others, but he was unable to catch the gist of any of the conversations.

It seemed much of the crowd was dispersing. The scheduled meetings had all wrapped up. Ron checked himself in the middle of cursing his misfortune. He noticed that there was a medium-sized group that seemed to be waiting for something else to begin. One of the elder members of the group happened to look in Ron's direction. He seemed familiar to Ron, but Ron could not place him immediately. He reminded Ron of an older version of one of his university professors, but could it be him here? *Why not?* Ron finally decided. *This is an academic conference.* Ron recalled his university days when in the midst of the crazy schedule of a medical student he had taken an ethics course to satisfy an elective. Although he had done poorly in the course, he remembered the value of it, and the fascinating professor. Now he wished he had invested more time in the subject matter, but maybe the course was about to pay off.

Dr. Stephen Hodge was a man in his early sixties, his age only recently beginning to show by way of a receding hairline and gray strands in his beard. The last Ron had heard, after many years as one of the University of Toronto's most respected professors, Hodge had become the head of its Philosophy department, one of the largest in North America. Moreover, Ron remembered that he was trained in Law and had practiced as a trial lawyer for twelve years.

Ron stepped up to the group, hesitated for a moment, then introduced himself to his former professor.

"Excuse me. Dr. Hodge?"

"Yes. How may I help you?" Hodge seemed almost to welcome the distraction.

"My name is Ron Grey. I'm sure you don't remember me, but I was a student of yours at the University of Toronto," Ron said, feeling a bit ridiculous yet also sensing a connection.

"Grey, you say? Well it's always a pleasure seeing a former student. I must say, I've had so many I don't remember all of you. But a pleasure nonetheless! Have you enjoyed the seminars?"

"Actually I recently flew in to visit a friend whose situation is relevant to the conference. But unfortunately I didn't find out about this event until too late. I just got here."

"That's unfortunate. That is, both that you missed the conference and about your friend. What is his predicament?"

Ron wondered how much information would be too much. "He has ALS, and the symptoms have progressed to the point where his quality of life is deteriorating at an uncomfortable rate."

"Well, if all goes well this week, he may have some choices he didn't have before."

"So I hear. I wish I could better advise him, or at least understand what he is experiencing. What is the possibility you might be able to discuss some of the issues with me?"

"As much as I'd like to, Ron, I'll be speaking at the senate hearing tomorrow and I must prepare for it." Hodge paused and then spoke quickly with a woman beside him, who left immediately. "However, I think I can offer you some kind of insight into the issues. We're about to begin the annual meeting for Academics for Social Justice. We'll be presenting a pretty strong argument on one side of the case. I believe there will be room for you if you'd like."

"I—I don't know what to say . . . thank you! I'd be honored."

"Great. We better be off; it's starting in a few minutes."

* * *

The meeting was held right on schedule at two o'clock in a conference room on the third floor. In the center of the room was a shiny oak table that looked like it would never end. Ron counted thirty-one people around the table including himself.

The room was buzzing with energy. Hodge managed to introduce Ron casually to the people he would be sitting next to, but there would be little time for small talk. A stern-looking woman, who Ron soon discovered was the secretary of the association, called the meeting to order, and slowly the room quieted down. During the secretary's preliminary introductions Ron discovered that Hodge was the senior editor of the *Journal of Legal Philosophy*. He also happened to be the president of Academics for Social Justice, which, Ron learned, was a conglomerate of some of the brightest and most powerful academics on the continent. Its chief aim was to research, debate and provide well-thought out solutions to troubling social problems. As the president of the group Hodge was also the chairperson of the meeting, and as he moved to the head of the table the room seemed to have a reverent hush.

Dr. Hodge began by briefly welcoming the invited guests without naming them and made special mention of the presence of a "former student" whose friend would benefit from the association's proposal for the senate's upcoming historical decision. Turning to his agenda, Hodge noted that although a number of items were included on it, today's meeting would be devoted to just one: the presentation to be made the following day to the state legislature. This was the pressing need, he stressed.

"We all know," he said, "that the legislature is conducting hearings and debating the issue of physician-assisted suicide as we speak." Heads nodded all around. "And we've been invited to make a presentation."

Light applause broke out. "Hear! Hear!" some of the members exclaimed.

"It is an opportunity that we are taking very seriously. As you know, this issue has been dividing society for some years now, and we feel it is time for cooler heads to prevail. We need data, facts, logic. Of course, mixed with compassion and respect for individual rights and autonomy." Hodge grew more animated as he spoke.

"Yes!" shouted a handful of members to Ron's left.

Battle language, Ron thought.

"And that is what we hope to bring tomorrow. We in the executive committee have been wanting to recommend to the government legalization of this service, and we have always wanted a strong, united front. As you know, we have polled you all via phone or e-mail and are happy to report that, without exception, you have all supported this recommendation. This allows us to make our recommendation unanimously."

Instant applause broke out. Even Hodge smiled. "Now that you know where one another stands on this issue, let's drink to that . . . later!" he added wryly.

Suddenly a slight man with jet-black hair who was sitting across the table from Hodge raised his hand. "Tom," Hodge acknowledged.

The man leaned forward, pulling off his glasses and looking intently at Hodge. "What is the exact wording of our recommendation?" he asked. "Since I voted for it, it would be nice to know exactly what I'm supporting."

This amused Hodge, and he smiled again. "Julie, can we hear the recommendation, such as it is?" Hodge asked in reply, glancing in the direction of a plain-looking woman on his right. "We're still working on it and will be until late this evening."

"Of course," replied the woman, opening a file before her and shuffling through a few papers. "We are declaring that people who believe their suffering is too great have the moral right and should have the legal right to receive a

The fundamental contention of those favoring PAS

physician's assistance in ending their lives gently and peacefully. Don't worry," she added. "It'll be embellished by tomorrow. You might not even recognize it." Light laughter was heard around the table.

"And we're anticipating objections," she continued. "The slippery-slope objection, potential abuses, that sort of thing. We'll be recommending certain safeguards to contain abuses and prevent a slippery slope."

Hodge was obviously appreciative. "You should all know how much work Julie and her team have done on this recommendation and the possible objections. It's in good hands, I assure you."

Applause broke out around the table as people nodded their personal thanks to Julie. "Remember," Hodge continued, "we're not the only ones invited to speak to this issue. Not Dead Yet will be there. The archbishop himself has been given time to address the legislators. A group sitting together to Ron's right shook their heads. "What's he doing there?" they muttered. "Why doesn't he stick to his own turf? It's a sad day when religious leaders start forcing public policy."

Should religion influence social policy?

"He has a right to be there and he will be there," Hodge stated flatly, overhearing their muttering "whether you or I like it or not. Who knows, he may have some worthwhile comments. He's an educated man, and you can bet they'll treat him with kid gloves. Physicians for Compassionate Care also has a delegation coming, and all of these groups will speak against our recommendation, and all will mention the slippery slope. It's effective. It scares people. The thought of children being euthanized, or the elderly even when they don't want it, or of teenagers asking for assisted suicide, or of people who are not even physically ill being euthanized. Scary stuff, and we've got to be ready for it. And believe me, we will be!"

Hodge continued, setting out the strategy planned for the next day's presentation. He and Dr. Patterson, the woman who had read the recommendation, would be making the presentation to the senate ethics committee conducting the hearings. She was a legal scholar with a list of publications as long as her arm. With great flair Hodge ran through the arguments that first he, then Dr. Patterson, would be making. This was to the delight of all around the table.

The room was filled with a sense of excitement, of mission and of purpose, and sounds of appreciation were audible as Hodge made his final comment. "The bottom line in all of this is that we want to put an end to paternalistic medical practice where the physician knows best and the rest of us are like children at the mercy of the physician's judgment."

"Hear! Hear!" was heard around the table.

"People want information, options and choices so they can participate in the decision-making process with their physicians. After all, whose life is it? And that, colleagues, is what it's all about. Thank you for coming."

Instantaneous applause broke out again and gradually died down. Some of the members pushed back their chairs, picked up their files, books and attaché cases, and headed for the door. Others began private consultations with one another.

The man on Ron's right turned to Ron with an open hand and a warm smile. "Hi, I'm Peter McKinley. I don't believe we've met."

"Ron Grey. It's nice to meet you." Ron tried to be polite without being encouraging. He didn't want to lie, but neither did he want to give out any information that might suggest his clandestine reason for being in Chicago.

"Are you from the area?"

"No. Actually I'm from Winnipeg."

"Ah. And what is it you do there—for a living, that is." Peter's confusion at Ron's terseness was becoming apparent.

"I'm a family doctor." Ron tried to understate this as much as possible. When he sensed that the questions were not going to end, he used Hodge's impending exit and the desire to thank the president for his gracious offer as an excuse to end the conversation.

"Thank you, Dr. Hodge, for allowing me the privilege of participating in your meeting. I look forward to the hearing."

"You are more than welcome, Dr. Grey. Wish us luck!" Hodge offered his hand, which Ron took as they left the room together, then they parted ways.

6

———

The hearings chamber was large, with the senators' desks lined up in an intimidating fashion at the front, two feet higher than the rest of the room. The chamber was packed with observers, delegations, reporters, television cameras and security guards. Aides were running back and forth carrying piles of paper and talking on match-box-sized cellular phones.

The senate ethics committee, which was conducting the hearings, was known to be about evenly divided on this issue, with a few soft or undecided votes up for grabs. Those votes would undoubtedly decide the outcome of the debate unless hardened opinions could be changed by the sheer force of the arguments to be presented at the hearings.

Ron took a seat in the far left corner, six rows from the front. He had shown up early and watched as the crowd arrived. A row of people who were sitting in wheelchairs was directly behind the table to which Dr. Stephen Hodge and Dr. Julie Patterson had been led. The back wall was lined with priests and nuns.

As he sat waiting for the meeting to begin, Ron's hopes were high that he would hear some much-needed facts and arguments to help him with his decision. The atmosphere was electric, and security was tight. A few people were praying quietly. Others were boisterous, acting like the whole thing was a big party. Guards with guns visible were at every entrance, giving each person who entered an airport-style security check. This was an emotional, life and death issue, and nothing was being left to chance.

Suddenly the large oak doors at the front opened and the senators filed in, took their elevated positions and looked down at the people who had come. The time was 10:25; the hearings were beginning precisely on schedule.

A few preliminary comments were made by Senator Paul Ryan, the chair of the senate ethics committee that was looking into this question. He was a distinguished-looking man with silver hair who appeared to be in his late forties. His navy blue pinstripe suit was complemented by a red silk tie.

As head of this committee, Ryan had become an influential senator. Just last week he had told the *Springfield Sun* that he was leaning toward support of legalization of physician-assisted suicide. He did, however, have a few reservations and questions that he hoped these hearings would answer.

Ryan immediately called for the delegation from Academics for Social Justice, and Hodge and Patterson, already seated at the delegates' table, responded by nodding their heads. "Please introduce yourselves," the senator invited, glancing toward the cameras.

Hodge took the microphone and began. He was smooth if he was anything, and experienced. He had done this before. He was known as a fearless debater who could make an opposing point of view look not only wrong but also silly, while at the same time showing respect for and actually building rapport with his opponent. It was uncanny to witness. Anyone who tried to copy his style fell flat, and yet to him it seemed effortless. It was commonly said of Hodge that he could whip you and make you like him as he did it.

"My name is Dr. Stephen Hodge," he began in a deep, professional tone. "I am the current president of Academics for Social Justice. We are a group of scholars, mostly in law and ethics, with proven track records in our fields."

Subtle, Ron thought.

"Our business," he continued, "is to research, publish,

debate and teach on ethical, social and legal issues that concern us all. We represent academic institutions, law firms and think tanks across this continent.

"That is a very wide-ranging group of people and professions, Dr. Hodge," the chair interjected.

"Yes it is," returned the professor, "because the issues we deal with have many dimensions: philosophical, legal, economic, social, psychological and medical, to name a few. We need more than one perspective and we have it."

The senators nodded approvingly, and Hodge went on. "We have made it our goal as a professional society to work with lawmakers for whom these questions are not merely academic."

This amused a few of the senators, and they chuckled into their microphones. Senator Ryan leaned forward, "So you're leaving the ivory towers behind and coming down into the dirt and grime with the rest of us. Is that it?"

Hodge smiled. "You could put it that way, Senator. Our purpose is to make recommendations to lawmakers such as yourselves."

"And what is your recommendation to this body today?"

The room grew quiet. "We would like to begin with a question, if we may."

"Please." The senator stretched out his hand.

"We would ask you, and indeed all citizens of civilized societies everywhere, if there can be any rational argument for insisting that a person continue to endure pain, suffering and indignity when that person would rather die."

Re-asking the critical question: Can we justify refusal to help a suffering person die?

Senator Ryan nodded.

"You see, as you well know, there are people all around this continent who are suffering from diseases such as multiple sclerosis, amyotrophic lateral sclerosis, cancer, AIDS and various respiratory diseases who no longer want to prolong their suffering."[1]

"Yes, awareness of these diseases and patients is increasing, and we're glad about that," one of the senators interjected.

Restating the
second
argument for
PAS: *Killing*
and *letting die*
are morally
equivalent in
similar
circumstances.

"And here is the crux of the matter," Hodge continued. "At present, people who are being kept alive by respirators, ventilators or other life-support systems can ask to be removed from these systems. They can legally receive a physician's help to end their life of suffering by pulling the plug, as it were."

"Yes."

"Under present laws any patient can refuse medical treatment, including food and hydration, for any reason, even if this leads to death. This has been of tremendous benefit to people everywhere who no longer desire to linger on and suffer indefinitely. Each year 15 to 30 percent of dialysis patients choose this way of ending life."

Senators all across the front of the room were nodding, knowing this to be the case. To some others in the room, however, this statement from Hodge came as a surprise, and they were obviously taken aback by it.

"Is that true?" whispered a man in front of Ron to his neighbor. "Can doctors do that?" The other man shrugged and raised both hands.

Hodge continued. "These patients need a physician's help because without that help, their death could involve painful and needless problems. And they get the help. This assures them of a hygienic and painless death."

"In other words," cut in another senator, "you are telling us that patients can legally pull the plug or be removed from a life-support system with the aid of a physician."

"That is correct, sir," Hodge said, looking directly at the senator, "but that is where the good news ends. In other cases where there is no respirator or ventilator to switch off, no plug to pull, patients are forced to go on enduring pain and suffering they do not wish to endure." His voice was rich and moved high and low with a dramatic flair. "The unanimous recommendation of our professional body is that these people, too, have a moral right and should be given a legal right to request and receive a physician's assistance in ending their life of suffering gently and peacefully. If this means actively taking additional steps to end life at the patient's request, then so be it."

"I assume you mean a lethal injection?" Senator Ryan inquired.

"If that is appropriate, yes. At present, physicians are already taking steps, necessary steps," he emphasized, "at their patients' request to end life, as we said. They are shutting off life-support systems, administering medication to render the patient unconscious and so on to make death painless and humane. We believe it makes no sense to refuse to help a patient to die who, likewise, is suffering and wants to die but simply has no life-support system to shut off."

"I follow you," replied Ryan.

"We see this as an inconsistency in the law. In both cases a person is suffering, is wishing to end life, and needs a doctor's help to do something to end life. Furthermore, in both cases the result is the same. The patient's life of suffering is over. The only difference is that in one case there was a switch to shut off. In the other, the only switch available is a lethal injection administered painlessly."[2]

The room had grown quiet, and people strained to follow the two cases Hodge had described.

"In our considered opinion," he added, "there is no meaningful distinction between these two actions. It is meaningless philosophical hairsplitting to say that there is."

This caught Senator Ryan's attention, and he looked at Hodge over his glasses. "Professor, do you mean that morally we should view them in the same way—administering a lethal injection and letting a person die of a disease?"

"Exactly," Hodge affirmed. "One is just as good or bad as the other. They are morally equivalent. And since the present law allows one but not the other, it is inconsistent and should be changed. Both actions should be treated in the same way, either both allowed or both banned. Of course, we think both should be allowed."

"Dr. Hodge," Ryan cut in, "did you say this recommendation is unanimous? Are there no dissenting votes among your members? Everyone supports this recommendation as you have stated it?"

"That is correct, Senator. There are no exceptions."

Ryan leaned forward, looking first one way at his colleagues, then the other. They whispered among themselves. This had obviously made an impact on them. These were researchers, scholars, people who studied the facts, arguments, implications and consequences of divisive issues and policies like these. And they were unanimous.

Hodge, clearly buoyed by the positive reception so far, carried on. "Senators, what we are talking about here is something as basic as individual liberty and rights, personal autonomy if you will. We are also talking about respecting the dignity of suffering people, and I ask you what moral right we have to force people to undergo pain, suffering, indignities or the loss of control that they do not wish to experience."

As Hodge was speaking, an aide sitting directly behind Ryan leaned forward and whispered in his ear. The senator was listening closely, the wheels obviously spinning in his mind. Then he leaned into his microphone. "But isn't there something missing in your recommendation, Dr. Hodge?"

"It wouldn't be the first time, Senator. What do you have in mind?"

Third argument for PAS: The possibility of abusing liberties—in other words, a slippery slope—is not a reason to destroy the liberties.

"Are you not concerned that legalizing this practice could pave the way for other unwanted practices? We've all heard that it could lead to such things as physician-assisted suicide for teens and for people who are not even physically ill but only emotionally depressed—and even to people being euthanized with no request. Others speak of a progression to infanticide."

Hodge nodded respectfully and put on his glasses. He then reached for a file near the bottom of his pile. His committee had worked late into the evening discussing this abuse objection. He waited for the senator to finish.

"Frankly," concluded the senator, "we're quite concerned about these possibilities, even those of us who may be favorable to your view. Would you care to respond to this objection since we're bound to hear it from other groups in the days ahead?"

A few people laughed nervously, wondering what the professor would say.

Hodge looked up at the senator over the top of his black-rimmed glasses and smiled. "You make a legitimate point, Senator. Abuses of any liberty are a very real concern that we take seriously. But the question we must ask is whether the possibility of abuses automatically constitutes a reason to destroy the liberty in question."

The senator raised his eyebrows at this last comment. "I'm unclear on this point," he said. "Could you give us an example?"

"Of course." Hodge had been hoping for just such an opportunity. He wanted to hammer away at this objection in any way he could. "Our laws grant us many liberties," he began. "Liberties like driving cars, flying airplanes, traveling from place to place and so on."

"True," the senator agreed.

"And each one of these liberties can be abused. A driver could ignore the speed limit. A pilot could disobey the instructions of the air traffic controller. The potential is there."

Senator Ryan was resting his chin on both hands as Hodge continued his thought. "But the possibility of abuse does not automatically constitute a reason to destroy these liberties. Instead, we look for ways of dealing with the abuses, containing them, and guarding our liberties."

The senators were all impressed. "Very helpful," said Ryan.

Hodge nodded and continued. "And we don't believe that the possibility of abuses from legalizing physician-assisted suicide is a reason to destroy that liberty either. Furthermore, we propose to contain the abuses of this liberty by carefully crafting the law with a set of safeguards, conditions which must be met any time a physician-assisted suicide is administered, just as we do with all our other liberties."

Safeguards: the way to prevent the slippery slope "Has your organization developed a list of safeguards it wishes to propose?" inquired Senator Ryan.

"Yes, we have, sir. Our recommendation is that a physician-assisted suicide occur only when the patient has an incurable condition, is in unbearable suffering and is in the dying phase, and when the request to end life is stated in writing. Furthermore, at least two physicians must be involved in the decision."

"And you are convinced that these safeguards will prevent the abuses?" the senator pressed.

But can safeguards prevent the slippery slope? An open question Hodge smiled again. "Let me put it this way, Senator. A slippery slope is neither predictable nor absolutely preventable, but we are confident that if these safeguards are followed, abuses can be kept in check.[3] There are abuses now under our current laws. We know that. We just don't know how many or how bad they are."

"But," the senator interjected, "doesn't that give credence to your opponents? In fact, isn't that precisely their point?"

"How so?"

"If abuses occur now, as you have just said, in violation of existing laws, then why should we think they won't occur later in violation of your safeguards?"

"Yes, the argument cuts both ways, and I have no crystal ball, sir. Our contention is only that the law must be changed to respect the rights and personal dignity of suffering people. That is the principle we cannot avoid. And safeguards ought to be put in place and enforced as best we can." Then he paused for a few seconds. The room was silent as everyone waited for Hodge's last and most dramatic statement.

Hodge closed his manila folder, took off his glasses and leaned directly into the microphone. "Let us always remember," he said, his voice rich in intensity, "that the possibility of potential abuses should never be used as a reason to deny people their rights and their dignity." Leaning back in his chair, he calmly waited for the senator's next move.

"You make a compelling case, Professor," the senator said, "and a thought-provoking one. I know your group has more to present in these hearings."

"Yes, we do."

"And we want to hear it . . . later," the senator replied. Glancing at the large clock on the back wall, he said, "It is now 11:30, time for lunch. I call for an adjournment until 1:30 this afternoon, at which time you will be invited to continue your presentation. He banged his gavel, and immediately reporters and camera operators rushed over to Hodge and Julie Patterson. A few also approached Senator Ryan, who appeared all too pleased to expound on the importance of these hearings for the individual liberty of all citizens.

Ron had to admit he found Hodge's case compelling. Liberties can sometimes be abused; Hodge had admitted that. And Ron had to agree that this possibility did not seem to be a good enough reason to deny the liberty.

Furthermore, he thought, Hodge was right. It did seem inconsistent to grant one group of suffering people medical help in dying but not the other group simply because the first group had the good fortune of being connected to life-support systems which could be switched off, leaving their bodies to do the dirty work for them. Maybe his decision would not be so tough after all.

Ron made his way through the bustling crowd to the main doors, which were now open and crowded with a throng of people all trying to beat the rush to the nearest lunch spots. Once outside, Ron hailed a bright orange cab. "Is there a Pizza Hut near here?" he asked the young man driving the cab.

"Five minutes away," the driver replied confidently.

Ron slipped into the back seat. The driver was a pleasant, well-groomed man wearing a bright plaid shirt. He talked nonstop as he drove, about the weather, the traffic and the hearings, which he seemed especially well informed on. "I'm with that professor they had on this morning," he announced. "Hodge, I think his name was."

Ron was surprised. "You mean you already know about him?"

"He's been on the news for the past ten minutes, short clips of what he told the senators this morning. Sounds like a smart man. The whole city probably knows about him by now. In my opinion," he carried on, "people should have a right to choose, like he said. I know this much—I would want that right if I were suffering, or in pain or stuck in some wheelchair."

Where have I heard that before? Ron thought.

"Of course," continued the taxi driver, "I feel for the doctors who would actually have to do the deed."

Ron found this last comment amusing. "Yeah, I know what you mean."

Would legalization of PAS place physicians in an unenviable position?

"It's sort of like capital punishment. Someone has to flip the switch. A lot of people say they are for it, but would they want to flip the switch?" He chuckled, shaking his head. "I don't think so." By this time the taxi was in front of the Pizza Hut, and the driver looked back. "Tough decision. I'm glad I don't have to make it."

"Yeah, right!" Ron said, paying the cabby as he got out of the car.

Inside, the restaurant was beginning to fill up with the lunch crowd, and Ron got a small booth in the northeast corner. Light music played, and a full shift of servers scurried about trying to keep customers happy, with varying degrees of success.

As a group of people passed by Ron's table, an uncontrolled elbow brushed Ron's glass, dumping water all over his pants. The constant hum of the restaurant quelled his quiet curse as he stomped off to the washroom. When he returned, there was a business card on his seat.

"Will Jones, Ph.D., Professor of Bioethics, University of Michigan," Ron read aloud. He studied the card carefully, flipping it over, and was relieved to see on it no indication of any media connection. A note on the back indicated that Jones wanted Ron to call him about something important. Ron shook his head and stuffed the card in his shirt pocket. Who was this man? Did he know Ron? How could he?

7

The sound of the senator's gavel interrupted the buzzing crowd of people and quickly brought quiet to the chamber. The time was precisely 1:30 p.m.

"Order please!" Senator Ryan barked into the microphone, and the meeting quickly resumed. Snatching a quick drink, Ron rushed over to a seat, this time near the main doors. "Dr. Julie Patterson, also with Academics for Social Justice," the senator was saying, "I understand you have some comments for these hearings?"

"Yes, I do," she replied, holding a pen in one hand and slipping on a pair of wire-rimmed glasses.

"Please, go ahead," Ryan invited.

Fourth argument for PAS: the democratic argument "Thank you, Senator." Patterson looked intently at Ryan. "First, I would like to point out that all across this continent people are demanding an end to paternalistic medicine."

"What do you mean by paternalistic medicine?" interrupted the senator.

(a) Refusing to legalize PAS is paternalistic. "I am referring to the medical practice where doctors always know best, and we, their patients, are like children, submitting to their better judgment."

Senators were nodding across the front, but Ryan was obviously not convinced. "Are doctors not trained to know what they are talking about, Dr. Patterson? Are they not the professionals in their field? It seems to make sense that we would submit to their better judgment."

A senator to Ryan's left could hardly contain his

intense disagreement with this comment. He shook his head energetically enough to be noticed by many in the room.

"Of course physicians know more about medicine than the rest of us, and their judgments are not to be taken lightly, but people today want options," Patterson replied.

"They want their physicians to help educate them so they can make choices, as many as possible. They want to participate in their own medical care. And on the issue we are debating today, there is a clear demand for choice." *People should be given medical options.*

"And you say that because . . . ?" The senator was moving his hand in a circle away from himself, waiting for a reply.

Dr. Patterson answered by reviewing a number of recent polls by Gallup, Harris and *Macleans* in Canada in which 65 to 72 percent of respondents claimed to favor having the right to choose a physician-assisted suicide. She added other polls from England in which the results were similar.

"And you are telling us that since the people want it, it is the right thing to do? Is that your argument, Professor Patterson?"

"Not quite," she responded. "My argument is that since the people in these democratic societies are demanding this service, it is wrong for others who don't want that right to impose their moral values on the populace at large. It is undemocratic, yes, but worse, it is immoral for a minority to impose its will on the majority who want to enjoy a particular liberty." *(b) It is immoral for a minority to impose its views on a majority.*

At this statement a group near the back erupted in spontaneous applause. "Yes!" one person shouted.

"Ladies and gentlemen," Senator Ryan cut in immediately, pounding his gavel, "we must maintain order in these hearings!" He paused and looked sternly over the crowd. "It is imperative that you hold all further shows of approval or disapproval until you are outside. The media will be waiting, and I am sure they will be happy to hear you there." Quiet laughter filled the room as he directed

Patterson to continue.

"Thank you," she said and then returned to her previous comment. "The majority of citizens clearly desire the choice. That is clear from the polls. And eventually the will of the people will be carried out. We are calling upon you, our democratically elected leaders, to do the will of the people now."

Senator Ryan was not enthused by her last comment. "I understand," he said lukewarmly. A few other senators, however, were nodding their heads in obvious approval. Probably supporters of legalization, Ron thought.

Patterson looked down at her notes, closed one file and opened another. "I would like to bring up another very serious reason why this service must be legalized," she said, looking intently at the row of senators. "And that is that keeping it illegal discriminates against our weakest and most vulnerable citizens."

Fifth argument for PAS: Refusing to legalize PAS discriminates against people who are physically unable to end their own lives.

This caught the attention of all the senators. "Discriminates?" inquired Senator Ryan. "This is a serious charge, Professor."

"Yes, it is, which is why we are bringing it to your attention. Whenever we see discrimination we must stop it."

"Exactly. But how does our present law discriminate?"

"By denying to suffering, dying people something that is legal and available to the rest of us."

Suddenly Ryan raised his hand to stop Patterson. "I'm afraid I'm missing something here, Professor Patterson. What are you referring to that is available to the rest of us but not to people who are suffering? Assisted suicide is not legal for any of us."

"But suicide is," declared Patterson.

"Of course it is, but we're not talking about suicide in general. We're talking about physician-assisted suicide." The senator was growing intense.

"Yes we are," she responded. "And if we insist on putting it in those simple terms, we miss the reality that the present law makes suicide available to the rest of us who are able-bodied but not to people who are suffering and unable to end their own lives. They can't do it. That's the difference. While suicide is not a pleasant subject, it is a legal option for the rest of us. Whatever we may think of it, we can and may do it any time we choose. They cannot."

"And you call this discrimination? Isn't that stretching the term just a bit, Dr. Patterson?"

"What would you call it, sir? We can do it. They cannot. How much clearer does it get than that?"

The senator looked doubtful but motioned for her to continue. "But it's worse than simply discrimination, Senator." *Where is she going with this?* Ryan wondered.

"Whether we make this service legal or not," she declared, "they're happening."

"What are happening, Professor Patterson?"

"Assisted suicides are happening," she replied. "Not always with the aid of a physician, but they're happening. Friends helping friends die. Sometimes with morphine gained illegally and administered poorly, sometimes with a plastic bag or a pillow. We're talking about suffocation or any other method that a person might use to help a friend die. And what is especially tragic," she added, "is that many of these are botched, and often with horrific results."[1]

Ron looked up at the senators, then around the room at the others. Looks of compassion and sorrow for these unfortunate victims filled the chamber, and he realized that Patterson was making an impact.

Suddenly Senator Ryan leaned into the microphone. "Professor," he asked, "do you have evidence of these botched suicides? Names, places, numbers of instances, that sort of thing?"

Patterson paused for a moment, then folded her hands and looked directly at Ryan. "Senator, that is a difficult and touchy matter because at present, as you know, this activity is illegal, so any specific evidence would implicate the people involved in helping others die."

Sixth argument for PAS: botched-suicide argument

Legal or not, assisted suicides will be attempted, sometimes with horrific results.

The senator shook his head slightly. "You are treading on dangerous ground, Professor." She nodded, almost defiantly. Ryan continued. "Let me ask you, and you do *not* have to answer this question if you choose not to. Do you, personally, know of any actual cases of this happening, and particularly cases where the assisted suicide was botched causing horrible suffering? Remember," he said, holding up both forefingers, "you do *not* have to answer."

The atmosphere was electric, and a hush fell over the audience as every eye in the room strained to look at Patterson, wondering how she would respond to this unexpected turn in the questioning. "I'll answer it," she said, undaunted. "No, I personally do not know of any such cases."

"Then why," he thundered, waving both arms toward his colleagues on either side of him, "should any of us believe any such cases exist?"

"Because they do, Senator."

"And this you know how?" His voice was shrill.

"We are in contact with a researcher in the northwest who, we believe, has scratched only the tip of the iceberg with her research."

"And what has your researcher found?"

"She has gone into the AIDS community and investigated as many as thirty cases where this has happened and has written them up in detail."

The senator nodded, shuffling through some of his previous notes. "And may I ask what your researcher has done with this information without implicating those involved?"

"She burned it."

"She what?" He was incredulous. Heavy murmuring spread throughout the room. "Order please," he called out.

Patterson continued, "That's right. She burned her research to protect the people involved, just as she promised them she would. With all due respect, sir, what would you have done?"

"Well I can tell you this: I've never burned my research and still expected anyone to believe the results of it!"

Patterson persisted. "And how else could she be expected to get the data?" The senator was shaking his head as Patterson continued. "May I add that she has been to court at her own expense for her research activities and her refusal to divulge names."

At that moment she held up a dark blue, hard-cover book with yellow lettering. "Here are the results of her research, of course minus the names, dates and places. We'd like to enter it into the record for your own future consideration. My advice, though, is to read it at your own risk." An aide quickly scurried over to Hodge and Patterson's table and took the book, then handed it to a person sitting at a computer near the front of the room.

"The way we see it, Senator," she said, "you have a choice to make. You can choose to believe the report of this researcher who has been willing to go to court at her own expense to defend the truth of her data, or you can throw it away. But believe me when I say that regardless of how you feel about this researcher, botched suicides are happening. Not even those who disagree with us about legalizing physician-assisted suicide disagree on that. It's only a matter of time before we all start hearing of cases of our own suffering friends, neighbors and loved ones attempting this terrible solution unless we act now to rescue them."

The senators looked grim. Some made notes, while others were obviously mulling over the believability of a researcher who would burn her research but be willing to go to court to defend the work and her refusal to divulge the names of her subjects.

Patterson closed the file she had been reading from and looked directly at Senator Ryan. "Our unanimous recommendation is that physician-assisted suicide be legalized to put a stop to these hidden, secretive tragedies. That way we can bring this activity out into the open, regulate it and make it more humane. To refuse would be to continue to systematically discriminate against our weakest and most vulnerable citizens, with horrific results."

At that point, Ryan took the gavel in hand and said, "I know you have a few more points to make to us, but I believe another recess is in order. It is now thirty minutes past two. Let's adjourn for ten minutes." After a quick strike of the gavel, the room erupted as pent-up emotions spilled out.

Ron jumped up from his seat and headed toward the water fountains just outside the large doors of the room. In what seemed like only moments the senator's voice was calling Julie Patterson to continue.

"Thank you, Senator." She had another file open before her and was holding her glasses with both hands. "Our last point will be brief, but we believe it is critical for the way this debate is being conducted across the continent. It concerns the way we have come to refer to the practice we are debating here today."

"You mean *physician-assisted suicide?*"

"Yes. We believe that the term is a misnomer. It should not be used here, in this context, for this practice. We are convinced that the word *suicide* is irrelevant to the practice in question here and that it is being used intentionally to distort the issue, to mislead people and to turn people emotionally against the practice."

"And exactly what term do you propose to use in its place?"

Is *physician aid in dying* a more accurate term than *physician-assisted suicide?*

"We think it should be called *physician aid in dying,*" she replied, "since this term more accurately describes what actually happens."

"Well," the senator chuckled, "I can see why you might not appreciate having the word *suicide* in what you are lobbying for. Few of us would." Many in the room laughed nervously at the senator's comment. "But just what is wrong with this term, *physician-assisted suicide?*" he persisted. "Doesn't the practice we are debating involve a person making a choice to end his life, a lethal injection intended to end that life and a physician's help to do it?

Physician-assisted suicide sounds like the perfect term."

"Yes, those are the similarities," Patterson conceded.

"Similarities, huh?" Ryan responded. "They sound more like identical features to me." Then he hunched forward and pressed further. "I have to be honest, Dr. Patterson. With all due respect to you, in my opinion this is not the high point of your presentation so far. It sounds very much like a game of semantics to me. The word has nasty connotations, so you want another word. Isn't that it?"

Patterson was unrepentant. She leaned into the microphone with her jaw squared. "No, that is not it, Senator! This is no game of semantics! We are talking about an attempt by some people to intentionally select emotive terms to slant the issue and to turn people against something they might not otherwise oppose. It is manipulation and frankly, Senator, I'm surprised that you don't recognize and oppose this type of deception yourself."

She's gutsy, Ron thought. *I'll give her that. How many people would say that to a senator, and say it publicly?*

Patterson then looked down at her open file. "You've stated the similarities. Let me point out the differences between suicide and what we are talking about here today."

"I'd like to hear them," he said, motioning toward her again.

"Correct me if I'm wrong," she said, "but when we think of suicide, do we not think of a person with a long life to live but who decides to end it? And is it not usually an impulsive act by a person temporarily overcome by depression or some other emotional problem?"

The senators hung on every word. People throughout the room were straining to see and hear Patterson as she spoke. This was a deeply sensitive issue that had probably touched everyone in the room in some way. She was touching a raw nerve with it.

Patterson continued spelling out the differences. "Normally," she said, "a person commits an act of suicide alone, often violently, leaving loved ones forever trauma-

Differences between PAS and other suicides

tized by the tragedy of the ending of a possibly long and fulfilling life. They are left with the guilt of wishing they had been there to intervene, not to mention the sadness and grief they also feel. They are left wishing they had known it was going to happen in the first place." She paused to take a sip of water. "But there is more to the difference between these two," Patterson continued. "When a suicide attempt is unsuccessful and the person is rescued, the person is generally glad to be able to live and thankful the attempt did not succeed."

Then Patterson's voice rose in intensity. "Suicide ends a living process," she declared. "What we are talking about here ends a dying process. We are talking about hastening a death that is already underway. The person has given it thought. It is what she would like to see happen. The decision is consistent with the person's values, and, please don't miss this point, Senators," she said, "the person would want to go on living if it were not for the illness or condition that is driving her to this decision. In a physician-aided death, there is no possible hope for recovery. The person's family can be there while she dies, and the dying person is grateful for the help she is receiving in dying."

She closed her file and zeroed in on Ryan. "Senator, I hardly need to say that a physician-aided death is vastly different from an act of suicide. That term should not be applied here, and when it is, we believe it is done to mislead and to distort. Thank you for your time."

Senator Ryan leaned back in his chair, his hands folded together. "Does this complete your presentation?" he asked, looking at both Patterson and Hodge.

"Yes it does," Patterson responded, "and Academics for Social Justice wishes to thank you for your time and your consideration of the facts and reasons we have presented today."

The senator nodded his acceptance of their thanks and then turned to setting out the schedule for the next few days' business. "Tomorrow we will break from these hearings," he announced, "since we have some emergency budgetary matters to settle. On Wednesday these hearings will resume at 10:30 a.m., and we will begin hearing delegations from groups opposed to legalizing physician-assisted suicide. On Wednesday morning we will hear from Physicians for Compassionate Care, an international organization with chapters in the USA, Canada and England."

Impressive, Ron thought. He had heard of this group but knew little about them. He had never been one to get involved in the political-lobby wing of the medical field. He seldom even voted.

"On Wednesday afternoon," the senator continued, "we will hear from Not Dead Yet, an organized lobby group of disabled people." There was slight laughter throughout the room at the name of this group. "These hearings are adjourned until Wednesday, 10:30 a.m.," he announced with a particularly swift slam of the gavel.

Ron worked his way through the dense crowd and thought of Patrick for the first time all day. Stopping at the battery of pay phones outside the door, he pushed in thirty-five cents and called him.

"I won't be back today," Ron told him.

There was a pause on the other end. "It's mighty quiet around here with both you and the media people gone," Pat eventually replied, softly. "When will you be back?"

"In a few days," Ron answered. "I've got a few more things to do here, and then I'll stop in again."

"I went into the office again today. Four hours. It's all I can really do," Pat said, barely above a whisper.

Ron rubbed his eyes and looked at the ceiling. "How did you feel?"

"Not as good as I did last week. My balance is off again. I didn't expect it to be this bad so soon. I hope it's better tomorrow."

"So do I, Pat. So do I."

Ron returned the receiver to its cradle and walked away.

8

Dr. Will Jones had not been difficult to locate. After the senate hearings adjourned for the day, Ron had returned to his room at the Holiday Inn and pulled out Jones's business card. It was 3:45 p.m. when he had tried the first number. The phone had been answered by a secretary in the department of philosophy at the University of Michigan and, yes, Dr. Will Jones was a professor in the department but was out of the office and classroom all week. He was attending a conference and doing research in Illinois, the secretary had been sure, but she had known little more than that. She had tried to be helpful. "I know he teaches bioethics, so it's probably something on that. They don't always tell me what they're up to," she had complained jokingly.

"I understand," Ron had assured her, then had asked if there was another number he could try.

"He has a cellular phone number," she had suggested. As she gave Ron this number, he had checked it against the other number on the card. The numbers matched. *At least I know who I'm dealing with,* he had thought.

When he had called the cellular number, it was immediately answered, and Jones invited Ron to meet him at the lounge in the Best Western, four blocks south of where Ron was staying. "Seven p.m. tonight," he said. "I'll be sitting with my back against the far wall."

***

The lounge was dimly lit and filled with small round

tables with a candle burning on each one. Seventies music played in the background, and numerous conversations were going on at other tables, making individual voices inaudible to anyone nearby.

A man was sitting at a table in the far corner. He was wearing corduroy pants with a light green sweater. His wavy, dark brown hair grew over his ears slightly and looked like it had not been combed since he had put on the sweater. "I'm Ron Grey," said Ron, extending his hand as he walked to the table.

"I know," said the man, putting down the cigarette he was smoking and clutching Ron's hand. "Will Jones. By the way, how's Dr. Metcalfe?" he asked without expression.

Ron felt the blood rush to his face, and he hoped the dimness of the room hid it. He tried to calm himself by taking a drink of water, but his shaking hand just made his anxiety more evident. "How'd you know?" he said, hoping beyond hope that he would wake up at any moment.

"I didn't . . . until now. I had Metcalfe on my mind from the news a few nights ago, and when a 'former student' of Hodge's mysteriously arrived at the Academics for Social Justice meeting, I took notice." Jones paused while the waitress brought him his drink.

"Can I take your order?"

"I'll have a gin and tonic short with a twist of lime, please," Ron stumbled. "On second thought, make that a tall."

Once the waitress left, Jones looked over his shoulder and continued, "I made sure to be close enough to you after the meeting to catch any other hints you might drop."

"So much for my attempt to remain anonymous," Ron groaned, burying his head and then trying to regain his composure as the waitress returned with his drink and a plate of nachos.

"Eat up, and don't worry. I think I was the only one at the meeting who knew all the guests. Anonymity is over-rated anyway." Jones took a sip of his drink to help a nacho go down.

"I notice you've been working pretty hard on keeping yourself scarce."

Jones looked up at Ron and chuckled. "I have my reasons."

"Which I don't suppose you're going to share with me."

"Actually, I am going to do just that, which is why I gave you the business card in the first place. There are some things you need to know." As he spoke, his eyes seldom left the doorway.

"Well your group is doing a pretty good job of cramming me full of arguments and ideas as it is, wouldn't you say? What else do I need to know?"

Jones removed another cigarette from the pack and tapped the filter on the table. "That I don't buy them." His eyes zeroed in on Ron's to watch his response carefully.

"You don't buy what?"

"The arguments for legalizing physician-assisted suicide."

Ron was taken aback. "But you're part of Academics for Social Justice, and they've just been sitting there for the past six hours telling God and everyone else in this city that their recommendation is . . ."

"Yeah, yeah. Unanimous."

The waitress returned with Ron's drink and a few napkins. After paying, Ron looked at Jones and said, "That's right. Unanimous. And they made a big deal out of it if you'll recall."

"Sure, who wouldn't want a unanimous recommendation with which to go before a bunch of legislators? They've wanted that for the past year ever since we heard we might get the chance to address the committee. The executive members have been in favor of legalizing physician-assisted suicide right from the beginning."

"You mean Hodge and Patterson."

"And three others. They were there. They've been sending us material on it for months: articles, arguments, cases, facts, that sort of thing, along with their own take on them. They've made it clear where they stand and what they hoped to recommend." Jones wiped his mouth with his napkin.

"But these are academics. Surely not everything they sent you was from one side?"

"Of course not. Both sides were covered. Proper academic fashion, of course, complete with commentary and evaluation from the executive members and their research assistants." He looked at Ron out of the corner of his eye. "About two months ago they sent us word confirming the date of the senate presentation. It was imperative, they said, that we have a unanimous recommendation to bring. Impact. Effect. You know." Ron nodded. "Two weeks later they polled all the members."

Ron took a large handful of nachos. "And you signed on in favor of it."

Jones nodded and lit up another cigarette. "It was a lousy day."

Ron leaned toward him. "Why not stand up for your view? Tell 'em you're opposed?"

"Because everyone else signed. I was the last one. They called me and then called again. Do you know how many calls, e-mails and visits I would have gotten if I had been the only one voting no? I would have single-handedly cost them their unanimous recommendation. I wasn't up to it. Gutless, wasn't I . . .?" His voice trailed off.

Ron didn't answer. "Why not just drop out, resign from ASJ? Who needs it?"

"I do, that's who." Leaning toward Ron and speaking softly, he said, "Do you have any idea of how prestigious this group is among my colleagues in the world of academia? It's filled with key authors, editors and presidents of other societies. Always has been. It's an honor to be a member. Great for promotions and respect in one's field. From the day you join, people begin to look at you differently. I've got a career to think about."

Ron was nonplused. This was nothing like what he expected to hear from the Ph.D. "So you went along?"

"Yep," he said, shaking his head ever so slightly. "I

didn't want to do anything to threaten my standing in the group. To be honest, I think they already suspected me on this one. I was the last to sign on for this recommendation and that was only after a couple of phone calls. I finally decided not to cause trouble and just to get through this one. They get their unanimous recommendation, and I get to keep my good standing, not to mention my friends in a highly prestigious body."

"So it was a trade off," Ron said. "Life is full of them. The only question is whether you can live with yourself."

Jones shook his head. "I like most of what the group does. We get involved in many important social issues. Race relations, environmental protection, urban low-cost housing development, corporate abuses in Third World countries, even cloning, genetic engineering and reproductive technologies, those sorts of issues."

Ron nodded.

"And normally there is the freedom to argue for any view you want to. It was just this one issue and all because of that presentation to the senate. They wanted their unanimous recommendation so desperately, and I was too gutless to stand up to them."

Ron took a long sip from his gin and tonic. He felt sorry for Jones. "Don't be too hard on yourself. I'm not sure most of us would have done any differently in your shoes." They sat in silence for a few moments as Ron mulled over what Jones had told him. This guy was a professor, just like Patterson and Hodge. He knew the issues, the facts and the arguments for legalizing physician-assisted suicide, and he opposed it. Ron spoke again. "Do you know what I really want to know?" he asked.

"What?"

"Why do you oppose the practice? You're a Ph.D. like the others. You've read what they've read. They're for it, so why aren't you?"

Jones looked at Ron and laughed for the first time. "Oh yeah, I've read the articles and books on it. Both sides. Good academic fashion. But then I decided to engage in a different kind of research."

"What other kind is there?"

"I visited a palliative-care ward."

Ron smiled at this. Here he was on familiar territory, or at least somewhat familiar. He spent much of his life in hospitals, but it had been some time since he'd actually stepped foot in a palliative-care ward. "And what'd you find out?"

A new kind of research: visiting a palliative-care (PC) ward

"That they were opposed to physician-assisted suicide."

"A lot of people are. What's your point?"

"I don't mean just the one I visited. The whole hospice movement opposes it. That's their official position."

"And you found that significant?"

Jones looked directly at Ron and paused. "You don't get it, do you?"

"Get what?" Ron asked, looking back at him without blinking, shrugging his shoulders. "I heard what you said."

"The significance of that." Jones's voice was rising.

"Well, then why don't you explain it to me? You're the professor."

"For most of us, this issue is purely academic. It's table conversation. We hear it on the news or talk to friends about it. We might even read up on it or write an essay on it. Academic theory. That's what it is."

PAS: not merely an academic issue for PC workers

"That's right. So what's your point?"

"That for palliative-care workers and the hospice movement there is nothing academic or theoretical about this issue. They work with people who are dying every day. They see them, talk to them, know them. You tell me who understands them and their needs better than palliative-care workers."

"Good point. I hadn't thought of it that way before."

"I've got a lot of respect for people like that," Jones continued. "When I found out that they all, virtually without exception, oppose physician-assisted suicide, it got my attention."

Ron leaned back in his chair and took another sip of his drink. "Well, it's got mine too, I have to admit."

"I thought it would, which is why you and I are going to visit a palliative-care ward tomorrow morning," Jones said firmly and finished his drink.

"We're going to do *what?*" Ron bolted forward.

"We're going to go to Southside Medical Center. It's here in Springfield. They've got the largest palliative-care ward in the city. It's already set. I made the calls and set it up this afternoon after you called me. They're expecting us at ten o'clock."

"Whoa! Whoa!" Ron blurted out, raising both palms toward Jones. "I'm not sure how it works where you come from, but where I come from people ask before booking appointments for other people."

Jones was unmoved.

"Besides," Ron continued, jabbing the air with both hands as he spoke, "I work in a hospital for goodness sake! It's my life! It's where I spend most of my waking hours! Did it ever occur to you that I could visit a palliative-care ward any time? I don't need to come to Illinois to do that!"

"Oh yeah?" Jones leaned forward and put his forefinger on Ron's chest. "So when's the last time you visited one?" Ron sat awkwardly and said nothing. "I thought so. That's the way it usually is."

"So you just assumed that . . ."

"I assumed that you needed answers," Jones interrupted. "You're the one with the decision to make. I may have been too gutless to speak out against my own group's recommendation, but I refuse to stand by and let a doctor who has to make the decision about helping someone die hear only one side of the story."

"So that's what this is! A guilt trip! That's why you dropped me your business card and told me to phone you. You're salving your own conscience!"

"Call it what you want. The fact is, if you need answers, you need information, and that's what we're going to try to get tomorrow. Can you be out in front of your hotel at 9:30 in the morning? I'll be by."

9

At precisely 9:30 on Tuesday morning a silver Chevy Cavalier drove up in front of the Springfield Hilton where Dr. Ron Grey was waiting outside. He stepped in and Jones pulled away from the curb into the light post-rush hour traffic.

"Mind if I smoke?" Jones asked. "The window's open." He nodded toward the driver's door window.

"It's your car . . . and lungs."

"Actually it's a rental, so I really don't care! Stupid habit, though. I've been trying to quit for years."

"I hadn't noticed."

The hospital was across the city, a twenty-five minute drive if all went well. As they drove, Jones sipped coffee and smoked two cigarettes and they made small talk. Ron had little doubt that this would be a day to remember.

It was a lovely day with no clouds and a slight breeze that had started during the night and chased away the humidity. They drove through the business section, passing hotels and service stations, then a row of stores and restaurants, eventually catching the main artery that would take them quickly across town to Southside Medical Center.

Moments before ten o'clock they walked through the double glass doors into the hospital lobby and down a long cool hallway where they caught the elevator to the seventh floor. The nurse at the desk politely showed them into the office of Dr. LeRoy Grange, the director of palliative-care services at Southside.

He was a large, gentle man with a contagious smile and appeared to be in his late fifties. He had practiced neuropsychiatry for most of his career but, five years before, had accepted his current position at Southside. He had a slightly receding hairline and wore black-rimmed glasses that he slipped on and off more times than anyone Ron had ever seen. He wore a white lab coat over a shirt and tie. "Gentlemen, come in," his voice boomed as he extended his hand to both of them.

After brief introductions, Dr. Grange motioned them to two chairs in his office. They talked about the senate hearings, which were obviously of great interest to him. "They could change everything we do around here," he said flatly. Ron and Jones realized immediately that his friendly, down-home demeanor concealed a deep seriousness about his work as a palliative-care physician.

"How?" asked Ron, somewhat startled at the categorical nature of his statement.

"Do you have any idea how many suicide requests we get up here?" He looked directly at his two visitors. They shrugged. "Lots," he continued. "They're a regular occurrence, virtually part of our routine. It's one of the palliative-care movement's best-kept secrets. We've come to expect the requests. In fact, they're one of the symptoms we treat."

Suicide requests: frequent after traumatic accident or discovery of serious illness

Then, slipping his glasses on, Grange opened a file and began thumbing through it. "Got one just this past week," he said. "A young woman who just found out she has terminal leukemia. Twenty-eight years old. Can you believe it?" He shook his head. "It doesn't matter how many of these I see; I never get used to them." He stopped and took a longer look at one particular page, then closed the file.

"Sad," Ron mumbled, knowing the feeling.

"And understandable," Grange continued, removing his glasses. "The suicide requests, I mean. Ask yourself. Would you want to live that way, knowing you'll never get better, only worse? It's not what most of us have come to expect out of life. We've all got plans, hopes, friends, family. This young woman has two young children at home. News like this is profoundly disappointing, and it tends to take away a person's will to go on living."

"How do you respond to a person like this?" Ron asked.

"The same way you or anyone else would respond to any other request for suicide," he answered without hesitation. "Why should the fact that these people are not able-bodied or healthy-bodied make a difference in how we respond to their suicide requests?"

"Hmm," Ron mumbled. He and Jones looked at each other knowingly. This was a rather profound idea even though Grange had said it quickly. There was no doubt that something happens in the minds of most people when someone they know is no longer healthy or able-bodied. Ron and Jones both knew that. When people like this request suicide, their requests are treated differently, as more reasonable or rational than if they were healthy or able bodied. Obviously Grange would have none of it. *The significance of the different responses to suicide requests*

"There is always some problem, some reason causing a person to want to die, and it's usually deep depression caused by something else. It could be a relationship gone sour, a terrible loss of a friend or loved one, an illness or the loss of some capability. Up here we respond to suicide requests in the same way you or anyone else would out there." He motioned toward the open window. *A common feature of all suicide requests*

Ron nodded as he began to comprehend Grange's perspective. "I'm impressed," he said.

Dr. Grange stood up and walked toward a four-drawer file cabinet on the south wall of his office. "These people's lives are no less worth fighting for than those of healthy or able-bodied people," he said, returning the file on the twenty-eight-year-old woman with leukemia. *Responding in the same way to all suicide requests*

Jones scratched his head. "But why prolong their suffering?"

"We don't," Grange said with great animation. "We have no intention of prolonging their dying process. We just want them to know that life can still have meaning and value and that their personal worth doesn't depend upon their good health or their capacities."

Ron leaned forward thoughtfully. "So you would regard a suicide request as . . .?"

Suicide requests should be regarded as calls for help. "As a call for help," Grange answered immediately, "just as you or anyone else would regard any other suicide request. And that's how we treat it. We respond with the best suicide-prevention measures available, just as we would for any other person. We treat their pain and suffering as best we can, and we're always researching and developing new ways to do that."

Jones was surprised. "But surely some things are different," he said. "After all, this is a palliative-care ward."

"That's right," agreed Grange. "Our residents are on a journey, a very difficult journey," he said, stressing each word. "It's a journey of ill health that will end ultimately in a walk through the door of death."

"Serious stuff," Jones muttered, looking up at the ceiling then slowly bringing his gaze back down to rest on Grange, who was twirling his glasses in one hand.

"In our culture," Grange said, "death is a hidden subject. We sweep it under the rug, act as though it's not real, and we definitely do not like to talk about it."

Death: a hidden subject "You have to admit it is a morbid topic," Jones said. "It's not my first choice."

"Around here we are open about it. We know our residents are on that journey, and they know it, and we are here to make the journey with them. We want it to be as comfortable and free of suffering as possible. People like this have many needs: physical, psychological, spiritual and emotional, to name a few."

Jones was dubious. "And you can meet them all?"

Grange smiled. "Of course not, but we sure try. Our methods are pretty comprehensive, if you know what I mean. We use pain-management methods, spiritual advisors, family members, meaningful activities and a variety of other means to meet as many needs as we can."

"So you don't grant them death with dignity?"

At this the director laughed loudly, causing the people in the next office to turn and look at them through the window, smirking. After a moment Grange's expression became serious once again. "That expression, death with dignity, would be funny," he said expressively, "if it weren't so serious. It's one of the biggest misnomers foisted upon the general public in a long time, the idea that giving people a chance to end their own lives is giving them death with dignity." *Death with dignity—an alternative definition*

Jones leaned forward, uncrossing his legs. "But surely, you can't be opposed to dignity."

"Heavens no!" he boomed. "We respect human dignity. It's what we are all about. But it's simply false to think we should express our respect by helping people end their lives when they're facing a difficult circumstance."

"Well then, what is dignity?" Jones persisted.

Grange leaned back in his office chair and paused. "That's a good question. It's also precisely the problem. In this society we seem to think that dignity means control over how, when and with whom we die, as though somehow control of our lives and deaths equals dignity." (a) Not necessarily *controlling* the circumstances of one's death

"But that's an illusion. Are we to believe that people who find themselves in wheelchairs or concentration camps are automatically losing their dignity simply because they are losing control over their lives? I've seen people come in here who are losing control by the day. And some of them face their circumstances and loss of control with greater dignity than do many people who are not residents here. They respond with gentleness, kindness, courage and decency. That," he said, leaning toward them and sounding more like a lecturer than a director of a palliative-care ward, "is dignity. These people die with true dignity. Dignity is in the response to difficult circumstances, not in simply having control over one's circumstances." (b) Responding with decency and courage even when control is lost

Grange pushed his chair back and got up and walked over to a coffee urn on a table in the far corner of his office. "Coffee, either of you?" he offered. After serving them both, he slowly walked back toward the desk. "There's something else," he said, taking a sip from his coffee.

"What's that?" Jones asked.

"We can't legally help anyone die anyway. At least not yet. We'll see what happens in a few days, when they vote."

Ron leaned toward Grange. "But according to Will here, you're hoping it won't be legalized."

"That's right," he affirmed without hesitation. "We hope physician-assisted suicide does not become a legal and available option for people here or anywhere else."

Ron was struck by the conviction with which he spoke. "Why not?"

The effect on palliative care of legalizing PAS

"For one thing, if it is legalized, palliative care as an enterprise will fold its tents," he answered matter-of-factly.

Ron chuckled to himself. This guy didn't waste time coming to his point. "That's pretty categorical," he said. "How can you be so sure?"

Grange looked at him then walked over to the file cabinet again. "Have you ever wondered how much palliative care is offered in the Netherlands, where physician-assisted suicide has been practiced for twenty-five years?"

"I've thought about it. Never looked into it," Ron replied.

Grange walked to the file cabinet again, slipped his black-rimmed glasses on and pulled out another file. "It's undeveloped compared to North American hospitals."

"Says who?" Jones inquired.

Grange glanced up at him over the top of his glasses and began leafing through the contents of the file. He lifted one article and began perusing it. "Here is one piece of research on Dutch hospitals, stating that in some of them there is not even a functioning pain team while there *is* ample opportunity to discuss one's euthanasia options."[1]

Ron winced. "Not a pretty picture. Lots of help in dying but not much in treating one's pain or suffering."

"True, and there's no mystery here," Grange added. "It's not hard to see why it turns out that way. When people come here, as I said, requests to die are frequent. Our present response is to address their depression, self-esteem, pain, suffering and so on, and to show them that even in this condition their lives are worth living. They still have value and purpose. Their value is not dependent upon their health or capabilities."

"Sounds laudable," Ron said.

"But suppose everyone who asked for suicide got it, either right away or after a short waiting period as euthanasia advocates normally claim they would require. Many of these patients would end their lives before the palliative-care service could even be offered or completed."

"Yeah, I suppose they would," Jones said.

"Which would reduce the need for palliative care," Grange continued.

"Uh-huh."

"And as the need for palliative care diminished, so would the resources and funding poured into it. It doesn't take a genius to figure out that when you cut back the resources, you also reduce the effectiveness of services, and you certainly cut back further research and the development of even better palliative care."

"Sounds to me like a vicious cycle," Jones muttered.

"It's a cycle all right, a downward spiral, and it ends with us being less able to address the needs of incoming patients, thereby pushing more of them to see suicide as the only realistic option. All I can say is I hope we don't go there. The better the palliative-care option, the fewer people will see the need to choose suicide."

Suddenly Grange jumped up from his desk. "Let's take a walk." They headed out through the doors and turned right, heading north past a small kitchen into a brightly decorated activities area. Ron noticed a small set of bookshelves full of various kinds of reading material on one wall and a stack of games on a desk beside them. In the center of the room one man and three women were playing a game of cards. They were quiet but seemed to be enjoying their game.

Ron's medical training had included no palliative-care component, and he had spent very little time on such wards since his graduation twenty-two years earlier. Jones, the university professor, was not a medical person at all, and even though he had visited a palliative-care ward earlier and was the one who had arranged this visit, he was out of his element and obviously uncomfortable. As they walked down the hallway, residents stopped what they were doing and looked up at the two visitors, studying them as though they were from some other world, making Jones even more uncomfortable.

Grange explained how the activities room was used, its purpose and the kinds of activities that usually happened there. Jones turned to Grange and motioned to the people in the room. "All these people," he asked, meekly. "Dying, right?"

"That's right," Grange said gently. "It's why they're here. They're on that journey, and we're making it with them." Then Grange walked over to one of the women playing cards. She was shuffling the deck slowly. "Hi Millie," he said, cheerfully. Millie slowly turned to look at him.

"Hi Doctor," she replied.

"How's your pain today?" he asked.

"Haven't got any."

"Good!" he said enthusiastically with that rich, deep voice, patting her gently on the shoulder. "We've been working on that for a few days," he explained, "experimenting with various amounts of morphine, and it looks like we've finally got it right . . . at least for now. We'll keep on it." Millie returned to her card game.

The trio walked slowly down the hall past a group of small rooms where residents lived. As Ron peered through the doorways, he could see some people in beds, others in soft reclining chairs and a few in wheelchairs. In some of the rooms family members were visiting, and in others residents were reading, listening to music or watching television.

Every time Grange caught sight of a resident, he would greet the person enthusiastically, often by name. He introduced a few residents to Ron and Jones. At the end of the hall they turned left and continued walking. There were more rooms, more residents, more visiting family members and a minister talking softly with one frail woman.

"It was a real eye opener coming to work here," Grange said intently to his two visitors.

"How's that?" Jones asked.

"Let's just say I learned a few things. Important things."

"About?"

"This thing called personal choice, for one thing, or individual autonomy. Isn't that what the professor called it on Monday at the hearings?"

Ron perked up. That had been Hodge's most basic argument, that legalizing physician-assisted suicide is simply a matter of giving people a choice to end their suffering. "What did you learn about it?"

"I discovered that we don't always do people a favor by giving them more choices. Wasn't that Hodge's point? Just give these people the choice, as if the more choices we give them the better off they will be?"

Giving people more choices: not always a favor

"Yes, that was his point. What's wrong with it?"

"It's not true, that's what's wrong with it." Grange's voice began to rise. "The professor is dreaming, and it doesn't take long working in a place like this to find that out."

Ron was taken aback. "Are you serious? I thought Hodge made sense."

"I'm dead serious," he stated emphatically as they rounded the next corner and began heading south. "And there's no mystery here either. It's true in all walks of life."

Ron was growing impatient. "You are making some pretty bold statements, if you don't mind me saying so.

Would you mind explaining yourself?"

Grange turned to face Ron directly and asked, "Have you ever heard of downsizing, or what do we call it now, rightsizing? Boy, there's a euphemism," he laughed.

"Yeah, I've heard of it, but what does that have to do with . . . ? Are we changing subjects here?"

"Stick with me," Grange replied. "What happens when a corporation downsizes?"

"People lose their jobs. That's what happens. It's not a happy scene."

"And have you ever thought about the unlucky CEO who has to make the choice of which two hundred or two thousand people will lose their jobs?"

Ron had, more than he wished. His own brother was the CEO of Master-Polish, an east-coast corporation that had followed the increased-profits, increased-layoffs pattern. Just last year he had been personally called on to reduce his work force by 120 people. He still sometimes lost sleep over the trauma it caused the families of certain employees. "As a matter of fact I have thought about it," Ron said almost to himself.

"Then you tell me." Grange stopped abruptly and moved close to Ron as he spoke. "Is it a favor to that CEO to be given that choice?"

"No, it's a terrible predicament to be put in."

"Exactly!" Grange declared. "CEOs will be the first to tell you that they would not wish that decision on anyone. In fact, the response of most other people is relief that they don't have to make those choices. Sometimes the burden of choice can be devastating. Think of the political leader who is faced with the choice of whether or not to send troops into battle, knowing full well that if he does, some will die. Or even the parent who must decide which medical treatment her sick child should receive."

Ron grew weak as he recalled the parents of a very sick child who were in his office just last week wrestling with that very decision.

"These choices are burdensome, and life is full of choices that we wish we did not have to make. Let's get this one principle straight," he said with great intensity. "Some choices are burdens, not favors. I said *some*, obviously not all. It is simply false and naive to think that when we give people choices, we are always, invariably, doing them a favor."

As they rounded another corner they heard music coming from one room. Peeking in, they saw a small group of family members playing guitars and singing softly to a frail woman who lay, nearly expressionless, on her bed. "She's their mother," Grange smiled. "Elizabeth Johnson. She loves the music. It's the only thing she responds to anymore." Jones was visibly moved by the sight. He took a deep breath as they walked away.

Grange turned to the two again and grew passionate. "What's wrong with those academics, those professors?" he said. "With all their learning, their intelligence, their skill and research, why can't they see something as basic as that? Some choices impose great burdens."

Jones squirmed uneasily but didn't respond. Ron was still doubtful. "Look," he said, "with all due respect, I see your point about the CEO, and the political leader and the parents, but where is the connection with physician-assisted suicide? Are you telling us that by giving people a choice to end their lives with the aid of a physician, we are actually imposing a burden on them?"

At the end of the hallway they rounded the last corner. "You figured that out, did you?"

"Well, I don't see it. No one has to do it. That's the whole point of it being a choice."

Grange's eyes flashed, and he turned toward Ron. "And that is precisely where Hodge's misunderstanding is. And the media's too. It's what they're all missing."

By this time they had made the circle and had reached Grange's office again, where he showed them to the same two chairs and continued speaking. "Thanks to the media, most people see this issue as merely a matter of giving a few suffering, dying people a chance to end their suffering if they choose and as a fight against a few other people who want to take away that right to choose. That's the impression."

"And you don't agree with it?"

Giving people the choice to die: a devastating burden

"It's not true! It entirely misses the devastating burden we would impose on the weakest and most vulnerable members of our society by giving them this choice!" He was adamant.

"Who? How?" asked Ron.

"The elderly, the terminally ill and the disabled . . . people who happen to be the most vulnerable members of society. They are the ones most directly affected by the legalization this practice."

Ron got up and walked to the coffee table. As he poured himself another cup of coffee, he wondered about Grange's contention. If Grange was right, then this issue was not merely about personal choice or individual autonomy as Hodge and so many others put it. *We only pretend that it is,* he thought to himself. But was Grange right? Anyone can *say* that giving this choice to the elderly, terminally ill and disabled imposes a devastating burden on them, but what was this burden and how was it imposed? Ron had a hunch that he was about to find out. In fact, he would make it his business to find out.

10

Ron leaned against the wall by the coffee table and looked at Grange, who was sitting at his desk looking over yet another file that he had pulled from the file cabinet. "Tell me," he said, taking a sip of coffee, "what burden are we imposing on these people by legalizing physician-assisted suicide?"

"Do me a favor," Grange replied without looking up.

Ron looked at Jones and shrugged his shoulders. *Why not?* he thought. "What did you have in mind?"

"Go through a mental exercise with me," Grange replied, still looking at the file.

"Sounds OK."

"Put yourself in the shoes of one of these vulnerable members of our society, in the shoes of an elderly, terminally ill or disabled person."

Ron was immediately uncooperative. "I've always made a point of *not* doing that with my patients in my practice," he said.

Grange peered at him over the top of his glasses, making Ron feel uncomfortable. "Well now, isn't that interesting?" He sat back and folded his arms, looking directly at Ron. I suppose that is to help you maintain objectivity? Is that it?"

"Yes, that's it," Ron replied somewhat defensively.

"And I take it this objectivity is meant to help you practice better medicine?"

"Yes."

"And I suppose that this works by helping you make decisions with a clear, logical, unbiased mind? Is that how

Illustrating the burden imposed by legalizing PAS

it's supposed to work?"

"Yes it is, exactly. What is this, an interrogation? I don't really need this!"

Grange ignored the comment. "Well that's another thing I learned from working here."

"What's that?" Ron wasn't sure he wanted to know.

"That there are times when that so-called objectivity is not all it's cracked up to be."

"Would you mind giving an example?"

Empathy, not merely sympathy, is required to understand the burden of the choice to die.

"Let's take this issue, for instance, physician-assisted suicide. Until you put yourself in the shoes of one of these vulnerable people, you can never understand and feel how the world will change for them if we make this practice legal and available to them. So do it. You have to do it!"

"OK, I'll go along, but this better be good."

An exercise in empathy

Grange pushed his chair back, stood up and began pacing around his office. "So here you are," he said, "in the midst of the stress, the trauma, the discouragement that comes from facing a terminal illness or a disability, or maybe you're a paraplegic or quadriplegic from a serious accident."

Jones looked over at Ron and raised his eyebrows. "Don't sweat it, Ron. It's only hypothetical."

"Hey!" Grange exclaimed. "It may be hypothetical for you and for me, but it's not for a lot of people, and even you and I can't guarantee that this will not be our life tomorrow or next week. Can you guarantee that?"

"Now there's a positive twist. Thanks," Jones replied, not bothering to answer Grange's rhetorical question.

The plight of people living with a terminal illness or serious disability

"And here you are," Grange said, returning to the exercise, "living with the fact that you are now a burden and an expense to others—to family, loved ones and caregivers."

Ron had to agree.

"You need constant care," Grange carried on. "You've now become a high-maintenance person. You need trips to the doctor. The pharmacy. The hospital. You may even need to be fed or need help using the toilet. You know this is causing stress and strain on your loved ones. They are giving up time with family and friends to care for you.

They do their best not to show it, but you're not stupid. And occasionally you do catch a look of stress on one of their faces, and you wish you didn't have to be such a burden. The worst of it is that while you require as much care as a one-year-old child, the child has the rest of her life to return the favor."

Jones shifted uncomfortably in his seat.

"And that's not all," Grange persisted. "You're no longer making the contribution you used to. You've lost the ability to earn money. You're dependent on others for most everything, and you occasionally find yourself asking what happened to your dignity and your sense of self-worth. At times you feel useless. How could you not? That is your life."

Jones sat in quiet shock. "All these people," he motioned out into the hallway. "Is that their life?"

Grange nodded solemnly. "It is," he said, "and there are many others like them who are being cared for by family and friends." Jones shook his head and looked over at Ron who was taking one last drink from his coffee cup.

Grange remained businesslike. "And at that moment in your life, imagine us coming to you and saying, 'We've got good news. You can exit the situation if you want to. It's legal and available, and there are physicians ready to help you do it. All you need to do is say the word and sign the form. We may or may not have a waiting period, and we might need to bring another physician in on it, but that can all be arranged. If you can't sign it, we'll have someone else, probably a family member, sign it for you.'"

"Aren't you being a little unfair?" Jones asked testily.

"I'm being honest is what I'm being!" Grange's eyes flashed. "I'm not avoiding the truth with semantics and euphemisms. Whatever words we choose to use, this is the message we are giving these people, all of them, those who want to die and also the vast majority who do not."

"So tell me," Ron cut in, "what, precisely, is the problem with telling them this?"

Grange lowered his voice. "It places upon these incredibly vulnerable people the added burden of having to justify their own existence, if not to others, at least to themselves. And this," he said, "at a time when they feel useless, discouraged and a burden to others."

"Justifying their own existence?" Ron asked hesitantly.

"It's unavoidable!" Grange said firmly. "The world has just changed for them and from now on their own continued existence is a choice they must make and can be called upon to justify. We have given them the choice to die, and with that choice comes this huge burden, whether we wanted it to or not. And remember once again who we're talking about. Extremely vulnerable people."

Jones and Ron said nothing, letting the full import of this idea sink in. Finally Jones spoke. "How will this . . . this need to justify their own existence work?" He had heard this idea before on his visit to a different palliative-care ward and was eager to explore it further.

Grange replied without hesitation. "People like this can be asked why, when other people are choosing physician-assisted suicide, giving up their medical equipment for others and ending the burden and expense on family and society, why they would like to live on—as, of course, the vast majority will want to do. And don't forget," he raised his forefinger and stopped pacing for a moment, "that some people in your line of work," he pointed toward Jones, "are already talking about a duty to die for people whose time is up."

Ron nearly choked on his coffee while Jones simply nodded, knowing full well that a number of philosophers and influential people were openly discussing it. He had even recently read a published article on the topic. This was no alarmist rhetoric.[1]

"And that's not all. Some people in the medical profession have already spoken of another possible benefit that could come from making physician-assisted suicide legal and available: harvesting organs for others."[2]

This was also new to Ron, but Jones was well aware of

Giving people the choice to die imposes the burden of having to justify one's own existence.

Is there a duty to die?

it. "So here you are, vulnerable—in fact, more vulnerable than ever before. And we come along and offer you the legal option of exiting the situation and ending the burden on others."

At this point Grange stopped and walked behind his desk again. Looking at both of them, he said softly, "I know for a fact that people who are dependent upon others almost universally feel grief and pain over the burden they are to their families. The sense of obligation to exit the situation, if it becomes a legal possibility, will be overwhelming."[3]

"You know that?" Jones pressed.

"Here is what I know," he said, suddenly speaking softly and intensely. "The infirm, the old and the dying are very, very quick to ruminate on their own uselessness and the burden they are creating for others."

Jones was very curious. "You've seen that?"

"We all have. Anyone working here knows that full well. People like these are also extremely vulnerable emotionally. Even the most subtle pressure from health-care staff or family to opt for euthanasia might remove a patient's desire to go on living." Something about Grange's last statement did not sit well with Jones, and he made a mental note of it.

"You're right," said Ron, knowingly. "Most people don't know this. How could they? Most people don't work in places like this, and very few of us take our elderly parents into our homes anymore as certain other cultures around the world do. We simply don't know much about the feelings and needs of the elderly, the sick and the very ill."

"Which is why," said Grange, "we need the present laws prohibiting physician-assisted suicide. They are pillars of protection for these people. At present they know they will be kept alive by default. No decision to live need be made because the issue never comes up. No justification is necessary for why one ought to live on or deserves to live on. No discussion with others or even within one's own mind is needed. But once physician-assisted suicide

When PAS is illegal, people are kept alive by default.

is legalized, all that changes."

"But couldn't we construct safeguards to protect those people if PAS is legalized?" Ron asked.

Grange looked up. "Ah yes, safeguards."

Could safeguards prevent the feeling of obligation to die? "Why not?" Ron persisted. "Couldn't we carefully craft the law in just such a way that we could prevent this abuse, or any other abuses for that matter?"

Grange slipped off his glasses and began twirling them again. "In safeguards we trust. Safeguards are their ultimate hope."

"Whose?"

"The advocates of physician-assisted suicide. They've put all their eggs in this basket. It's the way they hope to prevent all the abuses."

"Hey," said Ron, "I'm only asking this because Hodge mentioned it yesterday."

"I know, I know. We had the radio on. But let me ask you something. What safeguards would you suggest to protect elderly and terminally ill people from an inner sense of obligation, or from pressure from family members or medical staff to choose euthanasia?"

Ron shrugged, so Grange began listing off a few of the most commonly suggested safeguards. "The person must be terminally ill. There must be a written request. Two physicians need to be involved, and the request for suicide must be persistent over some period of time."

Safeguards cannot prevent the feeling of obligation to die. Grange asked pointedly, "Do you see any problem here?" Ron didn't, so Grange continued. "Can you find a single safeguard there or anywhere else that could prevent dependent people from feeling an inner sense of obligation to stop being the burden they are to their families or caregivers?"

Ron had to admit this was a new thought, to him at least. "Nor could they stop people from feeling the pressure from others who are encouraging them to request euthanasia," Grange continued. "The problem is not with having safeguards. It is that safeguards simply are not designed to prevent this kind of abuse."

Ron digested Grange's argument carefully. "You've

thought of everything, haven't you?"

"Ha!" Grange laughed heartily. "No, not everything. Just a few things. Right now I'm thinking about lunch," he said, checking his watch, "and we've got a great cafeteria on the second floor. Just hired a new chef right from Italy."

"Yeah," Jones grimaced, "I've had hospital food before."

Grange laughed again as he led the way through the door out of his office and down the hall to the elevator. "Then you'll certainly be surprised by the quality of the food here. It's the closest thing to home-cooked I've ever had in a hospital."

"Sounds hopeful," Jones said with a hint of surprise.

***

The dining room was beginning to fill up as the three found a table in the southeast corner, away from the busyness and noise. They had come a few minutes early to beat the rush. The full-sized window beside their table looked out over a large, well-kept lawn surrounded by trees.

"Not bad!" Jones admitted as he bit into his chicken fettuccini.

"What'd I tell you?" Grange poked fun at him.

"You've told us a lot of things."

"Yeah, you've probably heard enough on that issue for a while."

"Actually, there is one more thing."

Grange bit into his meatloaf. "You surprise me, Will."

"It's about your comment upstairs just before lunch about health-care staff putting subtle pressure on patients to opt for euthanasia."

"Uh-huh."

"Comments like that make me suspicious."

"About?"

"Well, get serious. Isn't that stretching it just a little?"

Grange stopped eating and looked at Jones. "Stretching what? How?"

Could people be pressured to choose PAS if it were available?

(a) Doesn't anticipating pressure to choose PAS imply a low view of family members and health-care workers?

"You're saying that family members or health-care workers might actually put pressure on a patient to choose euthanasia if it were legal and available. What kind of health-care worker or relative would do that?"

"It may not be quite as surprising as you think," Grange answered.

"I'd like to be convinced of that."

"I'll confess I was doubtful too until I came across an article written by a researcher who spent time in some Dutch hospitals where euthanasia has been practiced for over twenty-five years."

"And what did this researcher find out?"

"Two things that I found astounding . . . at first. He discovered that family members, more frequently than patients themselves, request termination of patients' lives."

Jones whistled, shaking his head.

(b) The facts about pressure to choose PAS speak for themselves.

"And family, nurses and doctors often—that's his word, *often*—put pressure on patients to request euthanasia. In fact, half of Dutch doctors, randomly questioned, felt it was legitimate to suggest euthanasia to a patient. Imagine how you would feel in your weakest moment if your doctor told you that she thought you should consider ending your life."

Jones sat in stunned silence, shaking his head. He looked out the large window, then eventually back at Grange. "Who are these people? These family members? These doctors? Are you sure this is legitimate research?"

"It's written up in a respected legal and medical journal."

"You've got the documentation?"

"It's upstairs in the file."[4]

Possible motives for pressuring a patient to die

Where else but in the file cabinet, Jones thought, still in a state of disbelief. "But why," he persisted, "would family members request euthanasia for loved ones? You're not going to tell me it's because they want to get at the estate or cut medical costs are you?"

Grange leaned down to pick up his napkin, which had

fallen onto the floor, then replied thoughtfully. "I don't really know. How could I or anyone else, unless the person making the request décided to tell us?"

"Good point."

"I suppose it would be naive," Grange continued, "to think that there aren't some people requesting it for that kind of reason. Greed, selfishness, exhaustion from caring for someone who is very ill, or a desire to get at the estate before it's all gone in health-care costs. Sure, that's possible, especially when you remember that approximately half of all health-care dollars are spent on people in the last six months of their lives. But how many people would fess up and actually admit it if that was their true motive?" (a) Selfishness, exhaustion and greed

"True enough."

"Which is why we'll never know how many of those requests had that motive."

There was silence around the table for a moment. Then Grange spoke again. "Actually," he said, "there could be other motives behind such requests, perfectly noble, compassionate, caring motives." (b) Compassion and care

Jones looked doubtful. "How's that?"

"Just last month a family came to see me."

"You've had this happen to you?"

"Yes, I've had the dubious honor. Their grandfather was dying, and they were pretty straightforward about it. Of course I refused, but not because they were bad people or had greedy motives. Actually, I admired them."

Jones was not impressed. He leaned forward and looked at Grange. "You admired people who asked you to euthanize their loved one? Is there something missing in this picture?"

"No, there is not. They only wanted to end their grandfather's suffering, nothing more. He was dying of cancer. He didn't want to die. He fought the disease right to the end. He wanted to live. But they loved him, and it was painful to watch him suffer. They wanted to end it for his sake."

"So they asked you to put pressure on him to choose euthanasia?"

"Uh-huh."

"Even though it's illegal?"

"Sure, which is what I told them right away."

"I should hope so."

He threw his head back and laughed. "As it turned out the family backed off immediately, and we all redoubled our efforts to manage his pain, which we can do amazingly well now."

"I'm glad to hear that. Pain has never been my favorite thing."

"That's another thing most people don't know: how well we can manage pain today. No one needs to go on suffering in pain. Ignorance of that fact, I'm afraid, is what is driving people to desire physician-assisted suicide. They see it as the only way to avoid terrible suffering when they are dying. If only they knew there is a third option, pain management, which is what palliative-care is all about."

"Which is where you come in, of course."

"Yes, it's what makes this work exciting. In the file I've got a recent survey that shows that many people who support physician-assisted suicide actually would prefer excellent palliative care over assisted suicide if it was available. They just don't think it is. That's the message we've got to get out." Grange was growing animated, almost like a crusader for the cause.

Ron put down his fork and knife and leaned forward. "So a family member might request euthanasia for a patient out of greed, or they might do so out of compassion."

"Sure. Both kinds of motives are possible."

Ron scratched his chin for a moment and then asked, "But what's the difference, really?"

Jones the ethics professor glared at him. "What do you mean, what's the difference? You can't see the difference between doing something out of greed or out of compassion?"

Does this difference in motives for pressuring the patient to die matter to the patient?

"Ease up a little, Will!" Ron fired back. "Of course I can
. . . in one sense."

"There you go again: 'in one sense'! What are you saying, Ron?" Jones was adamant.

"I'm saying that the difference in motive matters to us.
We can sit back like armchair philosophers and evaluate
their actions ethically, even legally sometimes. And of
course, one motive is better than the other."

"So you at least recognize that. Congratulations!"
Jones's voice was dripping with sarcasm.

Ron looked at him and pointedly ignored the comment.
"But what difference, really, does it make to the patient
who is being pressured to choose euthanasia? Either way
it's still pressure. The motives of the person applying the
pressure don't change that, and they don't matter much to
the patient."

Grange looked over at Jones and nodded approvingly.
"Ron may just have a point here."

Suddenly Ron leaned forward and grew very intense. "I
just thought of something else."

"What now?" Jones asked.

Ron paused to select his words carefully. "Actually," he
said, "could it be that the compassionate motives are the
worse ones as far as the patient is concerned?"

"C'mon, give it a rest!" Jones punched out each word
individually. He was growing frustrated. "How can you say
something that rash?"

"Hear me out!" Ron shot back. "It's always easier to
resist pressure from greedy people. Just tell them where
to get off. They're wrong, and you know they're wrong.
But the compassionate ones, now that's a different story.
They love you, they say, and they want the best for you,
and that's why you should consider euthanasia. How do
you resist that? I think it could be the worse of the two
kinds of pressure."

Jones did not reply, so Grange seized the moment.
"Gentlemen, let's not forget the bottom line here."

"Which is?"

Could compassionate motives for pressuring the patient to die actually be worse for the patient than selfish motives?

"That whatever the motives, pressure is pressure, and legalizing physician-assisted suicide opens up very vulnerable people to pressure from others to choose it when they might otherwise want to live. I think we can treat our vulnerable citizens better than that."

Ron and Jones noticed Grange quietly chuckling to himself. "Would you mind letting us in on what's so funny?" Jones asked.

"I'm just thinking of a conversation I had with a young woman who came to see me a couple of months ago. Adriana Ball. A grad student at the University of Chicago who is writing her thesis on end-of-life medical ethics."

"So you were part of her research?"

"I and a quite a few others. She strongly advocated legalizing physician-assisted suicide. She knew I didn't and couldn't understand why, so she decided to come and ask."

Jones chuckled. "I guess you have to admire that."

"True. She wanted to talk face to face with someone who holds the opposing view. That's better than I can say for a lot of people."

"And what's so funny about that?"

"The question she put to me," Grange replied. "She asked me to imagine I had a friend who was dying and wanted help in ending her own life."

This amused Jones. "That shouldn't have been too hard for a person working in a palliative-care ward."

"I told her that, which just led her to her next question."

"Which was?"

Asking the
right question "She asked whether or not, if it were my friend, I would want that friend to have the right to end her life with the help of a physician."[5]

"And your answer was?" Jones was pretty sure he knew exactly how Grange would have replied.

"I told her she was asking the wrong question."

"Your tact and diplomacy amaze me, Doctor."

"Actually I said her question was incomplete. She was

missing something."

"Oh, that's even better. What was she missing?"

"I put the question back to her. 'If you knew,' I asked her, 'just *if* you knew, that granting that right to a friend would mean that many other elderly, terminally ill and disabled people would die out of a sense of duty to die even though deep down they would rather live, would you still want to grant that right to a friend?'"

"And her response was?"

"She was not amused. Actually she thought I was avoiding the issue . . . at first. The only perspective she had ever thought of was that of the few people who actually want to die."

"That doesn't surprise me." Jones said. "That's what most people are thinking of on this issue."

"And it's important," Grange continued. "Don't get me wrong. This is a legitimate concern. People who want to die have real needs. But it is only one side of the story, and to stop there ignores the host of other people who would also be affected by the legalization of this service, the vast majority of whom do not want to die."

"Is that what you told her?"

"Yes."

"And how did she take that?"

"The same way. Not well at first, and that's putting it mildly."

Jones leaned forward with great interest. He was accustomed to putting ideas to people that, at first, did not appeal to them. It was just part of teaching ethics to university students. "So what'd you do?" he asked.

Grange smiled. "I said, 'Let's take a walk.'"

Ron and Jones laughed audibly. "Where've we heard that before?"

"It works every time. She met some elderly, terminally ill people. People who do not wish to die but who, if this service is legalized, will have to justify their own continued existence at a time when they are more vulnerable than ever before. She talked with them, touched them and even engaged one of them in conversation about the puzzle he was working."

Jones was impressed. "Sounds creative."

"Hey," Grange said, becoming animated, "if we look only at one side of an issue, any issue, we'll arrive at a predictable conclusion."

"That's true!" exclaimed Jones the philosopher. "Did they teach you that in med school?"

"Unfortunately, no," he replied. "But fortunately it's common sense."

"Which is not nearly as common as you might hope."

"True, but it's simply not honest or even fair to ourselves to ignore one side of any important issue. And it's especially unfair to the people most directly affected by the issue."

***

At one o'clock the trio re-entered Grange's office. He had a little story to read them, he said. One more thing before they would leave. It wouldn't take long, and it made the point better than he could. Once in the office, he walked immediately to the file cabinet and selected a file almost without looking, one he had pulled many times before.

Opening it and slipping on his black-rimmed glasses, he began thumbing through the file, eventually pulling out a newspaper clipping.

"Where's it from?" Jones asked.

"One of the local dailies," he said. "Two months ago when the senate hearings were announced."

"Big news I'll bet!"

"The papers began commenting on them right away. You wouldn't believe the letters to the editor. This one caught my eye." He held it up so Ron and Jones could see that it had been written by an Esther Barnes.

"Who's she?" Ron asked.

"A local person who's turning sixty-five later this year. That's all I know. And she's been doing some hard thinking about what it could mean for her if the senate votes to legalize."

Ron sat down and folded his hands together, waiting for Grange to read from the letter. Jones was at the coffee urn pouring himself another cup of coffee.

Grange cleared his throat. "'Next year I will be a Gold-Card-carrying senior,'" Grange began reading, "'and I am very much alive. I do not worry about any of the normal aging ailments. What I worry about is people who advocate legislation making euthanasia law. If I reach any of the possible stages of debilitation, I will still be a human being capable of giving and receiving love and, I hope, still precious to someone. If I live to an advanced age there may be only nieces and nephews to look out for me.'"

Then Grange paused and looked at Ron and Jones. "It's the next part that got to me." His eyes again turned to the letter. "'Will I one day catch my relatives in an unguarded moment, with a look of weariness or impatience in their eyes? And will I then think, *They're tired and stressed out with my care. The law says I can get help to end my life, so I must do it for their sakes?* No matter that I may still have a lot to give, or that my allotted time is not yet up.'"[6]

Grange put down the newspaper clipping and slipped off his glasses. Pushing his chair back, he got up and began pacing behind his desk. "That is the other side of the story," he declared. He was more intense than he had been all day. "We can choose to legalize physician-assisted suicide if we wish. The stroke of a pen; that's all it takes. But what we cannot choose are the consequences of that choice. They will follow whether we want them to or not. They always do. And remember, there are consequences both for the few who wish to die and for the vast majority who do not."

11

At four o'clock that afternoon Jones dropped Ron off in front of the Hilton and sped away. Ron wasn't sure when he would see him again. Jones had not reserved a spot at Wednesday's hearings and had been noncommittal about his own schedule over the next few days. *And they call* me *the mystery man,* Ron said to himself as he boarded the elevator on the way to his room.

He changed into more casual clothes and walked to the cafeteria for a relaxing cup of coffee and a Danish. Scanning the paper, he saw nothing about the hearings. He headed back to his room to change into his swimming suit, then went for a quick dip in the hotel pool. The water was refreshing. It cleared his mind.

Back in his room after the swim, Ron called room service and ordered a sandwich platter and a Coke. After being out all day, he would eat in for dinner. The sandwiches arrived and he ate alone while surfing the TV channels. He also thought of Judy and of everything he had to tell her. After he finished his meal and prepared for bed, he sat on the edge of the bed and called her. In moments Judy was on the phone. "Hi Love!" Ron said.

"Ron!" she replied. Then she paused uncomfortably.

Noticing the silence, Ron asked, "What's the matter, Judy?"

Turning serious, she said, "I received a phone call today, Ron. It was ATN."

Ron's heart skipped a beat. "It was who?"

"ATN. They were asking a lot of questions."

"They called our house?"

"Yes."

"How'd they get our number?"

Judy laughed. "Are you forgetting? This is ATN. Investigating is their business. Finding our number was probably a piece of cake for them. They called your office first."

"The office? What happened there?"

"They talked to Ruby. She finally told them you were out of the office for a few days. Now she wonders if she did the right thing. She wouldn't put them through to anyone else even though they kept on asking. They even tried to get our home number out of her, but she wouldn't give them that either. My advice to you, Doctor, is to think of something to say when they call you. It's only a matter of time. I think we both know that."

"Oh great!" he said, frowning at the phone. Ruby was the new receptionist, and Ron felt badly that she had been put in this awkward situation because of him. "It's starting. What did you tell them?"

"To get lost."

"That's my wife. Tactful as ever."

"Oh, I chose slightly different terminology but I think they got the point. I found the person to be annoying anyway, so it made it easier."

Ron rubbed his temples and began pacing the floor as far as the phone cord would stretch. "It sounds like between you and Ruby, I'm in good hands on this trip."

"Speaking of this trip, have you made any decisions yet?"

Ron cleared his throat. "Now that all depends upon exactly when you ask. If you had asked yesterday after the hearings, I would have said yes. It seemed . . . well . . . almost obvious, then."

"The hearings were that good, were they?"

"It was the delegation from Academics for Social Justice yesterday. The two people were powerful. They agreed with Pat's decision and they gave more reasons for it—a lot more reasons. Good reasons that I'd never thought of. At least they sounded good to me and to most of the people around me.

"What's more, these people have studied the issues for years. They're university professors, and they claimed their membership was unanimously in favor of legalizing physician-assisted suicide."

Ron briefly recounted to Judy Hodge's and Patterson's arguments about the inconsistency of the present laws on euthanasia, the use of the term *suicide*, and the duty of legislators to do the will of the people. He explained carefully Hodge's response to the objection that the practice of physician-assisted suicide could be abused.

Ron had been strongly convinced by these arguments and told Judy so. She listened silently as the thought began to sink in that her husband was actually seriously contemplating ending the life of another human being. Then she spoke. "It sounds to me like your decision has been made. Mission accomplished. C'mon home."

"That was yesterday," Ron replied.

Judy paused. "OK," she said, very slowly. "And what's happened since then? I know the hearings were postponed for a day. That was on the news."

"I spent the day at a palliative-care ward with the director of the ward," Ron answered.

"And. . .?"

"I discovered a whole new perspective on this issue, new reasons all pointing in the opposite direction. They were powerful too, things I had never thought of, and I had no response to them. I also found out that the delegation the day before was not really unanimous. It was, but it wasn't."

"That sounds clear. How did you learn that?"

"I met the dissenter."

"How did you find him?"

"He found me. He claimed it wasn't too hard."

"Well that's interesting. And I'll bet he didn't have the resources of the ATN machine at his disposal either."

"That's encouraging, dear." Ron said. Judy had a way of

cutting through all the details, getting to the point and putting things on the table, warts and all.

Then, starting with his meeting with Jones at the lounge, Ron related the activities of the past twenty-six hours to her. He told her Jones's story about ASJ, and about Grange's argument that legalizing physician-assisted suicide would impose a devastating burden upon elderly, terminally ill and disabled people.

Ron's experience at the ward had moved him, and he told Judy so. "So now you're confused again," she said.

"You could say that. I've found there is a lot more to this issue than I first knew. I'm hoping the delegations tomorrow can help me."

Judy didn't know what to say but wanted to be helpful. "I don't really understand what you're going through," she said, trying to console him. "Take the time you need to get the information, and no matter what decision you make I'll support you. The girls and I are fine, really."

Ron had seldom loved Judy more than he did at that moment. He stopped pacing and sat down on the bed. His nerves were frayed from the weight of this decision, and his mind and emotions had been tossed back and forth. But Judy was there, a paragon of stability and love.

"I've got a question for you, Love," he said. "A serious question."

"Uh-huh." Judy wasn't sure how to react.

"I need your help," Ron said. "I need you to be honest. Not that that has ever been a problem with you, but I need brutal honesty."

"What is it, Ron?" she spoke softly.

"What if it were us?"

"What if *what* were us?" Judy pressed.

"Pat and Jean. What if we were in their shoes? What if it was me who had ALS and wanted to die? It could happen, you know. Who would have thought it would happen to Pat and Jean?"

Asking the personal question: What if it were us?

"What are you asking me, Ron?"

"I'm asking if you would want me to get a physician-assisted suicide. I need to know, Judy."

Judy drew in a huge breath of air and exhaled it slowly. "C'mon, Ron, you can't ask me that. It's too hard. This isn't fair."

"Of course it's not fair. I didn't say it was. What is fair anymore? Can someone tell me that? Is it fair that Pat has ALS? Is it fair that Jean has to watch her husband suffer, deteriorate and eventually die from ALS? Is it fair that I've been pushed into this decision and, as we speak, am being hunted down by ATN so they can broadcast my face into every home in this country as the doctor who is thinking of giving his friend a lethal injection?" Ron's tone of voice reflected his frustration at being unable to reconcile his inner conflict.

"Ron, please. I was just saying that . . ." Judy didn't know how to respond.

Ron stopped himself and took a deep breath. Then he spoke, consciously being more tender, "I'm sorry, Honey. It's just that although fair is a nice idea, it unfortunately hasn't had much to do with my day-to-day life for the past couple of weeks."

There was another pause. "I'll do it, honey," Judy finally said. "I'll think about what I would want if it were us. And I will be as honest as I possibly can."

Ron had no doubt that she would. "Thanks, Love," he answered, much more quietly. "You're a dream come true."

He hung up the phone, exhausted, and collapsed into bed.

12

The time was precisely 9:25 on Wednesday morning, and the senate hearings room was again packed with observers. Without warning the large oak doors at the front opened, just as they had on Monday. Ron watched as the senators marched in, took their elevated seats and looked out over the heads of everyone else in the room.

He had arrived early and grabbed a seat near the door, eight rows from the front, where he watched as the throng poured in through the double doors that were thrown open directly beside him.

He was struck by the wide variety of people who would choose to attend hearings like these. White collar and blue collar, young and old, people in business suits and people who were casually dressed. Some seemed happy to be there, while others were painfully somber. There were many more people in wheelchairs today than on Monday—rows of them directly behind the table where the delegates would make their presentations.

At the delegates' table were two people, a man and a woman, both dressed in business suits. They had been conversing quietly and thumbing through files, documents and even a couple of books, obviously having one last look at their presentation material. A full morning lay ahead of them.

Senator Ryan had taken his seat in the big chair in the middle of the row of senators. He looked down over his reading glasses at the standing-room-only crowd. With a swift rap of his gavel, he brought all conversations to an end. "Order please!" he called out as the room quickly quieted down. "Order! Thank you."

In a businesslike manner Senator Ryan welcomed all the guests and observers and proceeded to take care of a few housekeeping matters: the plan and schedule for the day with one lunch break and two ten-minute breaks strictly enforced, names of the upcoming delegations, the purpose of the hearings and so on.

Then, looking down at the notes before him, Senator Ryan said, "Today we will hear from delegations who oppose legalizing physician-assisted suicide, and we have two. Our first delegation is from Physicians for Compassionate Care, and later in the day we will hear from Not Dead Yet." A smattering of light laughter could be heard throughout the room at the mention of the name of the latter group. Ryan was not amused. He glared sternly at the crowd, which immediately became hushed.

"We will now hear from Physicians for Compassionate Care." Turning to the two people sitting at the delegates' table, he said, "Please introduce yourselves and go ahead."

"Thank you, Senator," replied the woman. "My name is Dr. Joy Buckley. I am a general surgeon practicing in Memphis."

Ryan knew this, as did every other senator present as well as a good many people in the room. Dr. Joy Buckley was well known as an active member of the American Medical Association and had become highly respected in the medical community. Her appearances on many national radio and television programs over the past six years had given her a national profile. She had made a personal study of euthanasia, giving seminars on it at the AMA national convention for the past three years, and was a natural to be leading this delegation.

"With me," she continued, "is our legal counsel, attorney Dale Vanzanten, who is a partner in the law firm of MacKenzie, Maxwell and Watson, which has offices in

Denver and New York." Vanzanten nodded in Ryan's direction. "Mr. Vanzanten and I will share this presentation."

The senators nodded their approval of the delegates' credentials, if not of their personal views.

Dr. Buckley leaned into the microphone and spoke directly to Senator Ryan. "We are an international group of physicians," she said. "Our members represent every medical specialty and have received their training at virtually all of the major medical training institutions on the continent."

Ryan smiled. "That's impressive, Doctor. So you're not a small fringe group of disgruntled physicians?" he said, trying to inject a bit of levity into the discussion.

"I'm glad you recognize that, Senator."

Ryan smiled good-naturedly, glancing toward the cameras. *They're off to a good start,* Ron thought. *I wonder how long that'll last.*

Then Dr. Buckley looked down at the file that was open before her. "Physicians for Compassionate Care," she began, "strongly urges you not to make physician-assisted suicide legal. On the contrary, we call upon you to keep the present laws, which prohibit this practice, in place. In our view these laws serve to protect vulnerable patients at the time when they need it the most."

The senator leaned forward. "I'm sure you know we've had another delegation urging us to do precisely the opposite."

"Yes, we are aware of that group," she said, "and its arguments."

The senator paused. "You were here when they spoke to us?"

"Yes."

"So you know what they told us?"

"Yes."

"And you are aware of their credentials, their experience and their expertise on this issue?" The room had grown quiet. People were leaning forward in their chairs to catch Buckley's answers to Ryan's mini-interrogation.

"Yes."

Ryan chuckled. Pulling off his glasses, he leaned back in his gigantic office chair. "I have to be frank with you, Doctor. We've found some of the arguments put forward by the advocates of legalization to be persuasive."

The necessity of hearing both sides of important issues

"I'm sure you did, sir. Any side of an issue can be made to sound persuasive when it is the only side one hears."

This amused Ryan and he chuckled again. "OK then, why exactly are you opposed to making this service legal?"

"Because while the reasons in favor of legalizing it have some merit . . ."

"So you admit that?" Ryan interrupted.

"Of course, especially when they are put as well as they were in this room two days ago. If the arguments favoring legalization of this practice were the only arguments to be considered, then we would all support legalization."

"I see. But, of course, you think they are not the only ones to be considered. Am I right, Doctor?"

"That is correct, and we would do ourselves a great disservice by not examining all the relevant arguments on an issue this important."

Arguments opposing the legalization of PAS

She paused, waiting for Ryan to comment, but he did not, so she continued. "As I was saying, while the reasons favoring legalization of this practice have some force, we are convinced that the reasons against it are overpowering. Thanks to the media coverage of this issue, they're also largely unknown. That is not because they are mysterious or especially profound but only because they are new to many of us."

"Well, you've got my attention, Doctor. What are these reasons?"

"I thought you'd never ask," Buckley said, laughing.

"Today it's my job to ask questions."

"First is the possibility of misdiagnoses leading patients who may not even be terminally ill, but who think they are, to request and receive physician-assisted suicide."

"Hmm." This was obviously a new idea to Ryan, and he was not expecting it. "What do you mean, misdiagnoses? You're scaring some of us up here, Doctor." He had a fearful smirk on his face.

Buckley looked up. "It may come as a surprise to some people," she replied, "but every physician knows that medicine is not an exact science. It is not mathematics, and the possibility of physicians misdiagnosing their patients is very real. It happens."

With the same smirk Ryan looked from side to side at his colleagues, shaking his head. People throughout the audience began to laugh. Not only was the senator a politician, he was also an actor. "Frankly, Doctor, that was not the word of assurance, or should I say, diagnosis, I was hoping to hear."

"At least it was free this time," she replied.

"Yes, that is a welcome change."

"And let me assure you," she continued, "that I and my colleagues across North America take great pains to get it right. Second opinions, x-rays, double checks, conservative prognoses. But the fact remains that we doctors are human, and medicine is not an exact science, and sometimes misdiagnoses happen."

"I feel a little better now . . . I think," Ryan said to the laughter of a few of his colleagues. "And your point is?" He held out both hands.

"That because it happens, it allows for the possibility that a physician may actually help end the life of the 'wrong person.'" She held up two fingers on each hand to imitate quotation marks.

"You're right, that *is* a new idea."

"And what makes this especially serious," she continued, "is that most requests for suicide come immediately after patients are diagnosed with a terminal illness, or after serious accidents when people are told they are now paraplegic or quadriplegic. That is when any of us would be most vulnerable."

Ryan looked grim. "Yes, I guess that kind of news could

[margin notes:] First argument opposing PAS: the possibility of misdiagnoses leading to suicide requests by people who are not terminally ill

(a) Medicine is not an exact science; misdiagnoses happen.

have a way of destroying a person's will to live, couldn't it?"

"It could and it does," Buckley replied, "which is why we should seriously question whether a physician's assistance should be available to these people to help them die if they request it."

Ryan again pulled off his glasses and leaned back, looking at the ceiling. Suddenly an aide directly behind him leaned forward and thrust a piece of paper into his hand. He cupped one hand over his microphone, and the two whispered together for a few seconds. Then he again spoke into the microphone. "Isn't this the same argument opponents of capital punishment use?" he asked. "Don't they tell us that executing criminals creates the possibility of executing the wrong person?"

"Yes," Buckley answered. "That has always been one important consideration in the capital punishment debate, and for good reason. Whatever one thinks on that issue, we must face the fact that over the years in this country we have executed a number of innocent people by mistake. It is almost certain that a similar thing will happen if we legalize physician-assisted suicide."

"How can you be so sure?"

Buckley thumbed through her file and pulled out a document near the back. Without looking up she replied, "Recently we came across this piece of information from the Foundation for Suicide Prevention. It surprised and, I might add, dismayed us."[1]

"Uh-huh." Ryan leaned forward expectantly.

(b) People who mistakenly believe they are ill may commit suicide. "In our society right now, even without physicians available to help people die, more individuals, particularly elderly people, kill themselves because they fear and *mistakenly* believe they have cancer than those who kill themselves and actually have cancer."

Ryan was stunned. "You mean they don't even have cancer?"

"That's right."

"And they're killing themselves because they think they do?"

"Yes. It's a hidden tragedy. And there's more. Preoccupation with suicide is greater among those awaiting the results of tests for HIV antibodies than among those who already know they are HIV positive."

(c) Preoccupation with suicide is high among people awaiting test results for serious illnesses.

Ryan's face reddened as he looked from side to side at the other senators. "I wasn't aware of the severity of the problem, Doctor." He was shocked. "Doctor, I'm assuming that something is being done about this—but if not, what in your professional opinion, can be done to rectify the situation?"

Buckley shook her head. "This is a difficult problem, Senator."

"I hope you can tell us more than that, Doctor!"

"These people leave our offices deeply distressed, believing they have cancer or AIDS, or at least wondering if they might have them, and knowing there is nothing they can do but wait for the test results. Every little bruise or stomach pain makes them wonder all over again if they are deathly ill."

"And yet, if there is a misdiagnosis, they aren't seriously ill at all."

"That's right. But waiting for these kinds of test results can be unbearable, and our words of comfort seem empty against anxiety this deep."

Senator Ryan grew very intense. "There's got to be something we can do." His deep voice ricocheted off the back walls and around the room.

Buckley scanned the row of senators. "There is something, Senator."

"What?"

"At the very least we can resist the temptation to tamper with the laws that are there to protect people just like these." Now the doctor grew intense. "The very possibility that a physician could help a healthy but misdiagnosed and deeply distressed person die is reason enough not to eliminate those pillars of protection."

"Do you mean the laws prohibiting physician-assisted suicide?"

(d) Keeping PAS illegal protects suicidal people.

"Yes I do. I guarantee you that people like this will be

eternally grateful for the protection when their misdiagnosis is discovered."

Ryan smiled at this.

"They are extremely vulnerable at that time in their lives, and frankly, Senators, they are in enough danger without us making it easier for them to make an irreversible mistake."

A few senators nodded approvingly while others sat stone-faced. Senator Ryan was writing but paused to look up and see Dr. Buckley closing her file and leaning back in her chair. His eyes darted back and forth between the two members seated at the delegates' table, and it soon became clear that the next argument was to be made by Vanzanten. He was sitting erect with a legal pad and a set of typed notes before him.

"My name is Dale Vanzanten," he began, "legal counsel for Physicians for Compassionate Care." His voice was high-pitched and not at all easy to listen to. It stood in sharp contrast to the smooth, bass intonations resonating from Ryan. His thick, jet-black hair was greased and combed straight back, covering the tops of his ears.

Second argument against PAS: the slippery slope—PAS invites other, tragic, practices.

Vanzanten leaned forward, looking directly at the row of senators, and began speaking into the microphone with the intensity of a televangelist. "Imagine a society," he said, "where people who are not physically ill at all but only deeply depressed can ask for a physician-assisted suicide and receive it; where any emotionally distraught teenager can receive a physician's aid in ending her own life; where your doctor may actually suggest that you consider euthanasia when you are weak and suffering, even though you did not and would not ask for it; and where people are euthanized with no request at all."

Ryan took off his glasses and glared at Vanzanten. "Mr. Vanzanten," he interrupted loudly, "this is preposterous, and I suggest it is an attempt to smear your opponents on this issue!"

"It is nothing of the . . ."

"I'm asking you to move beyond this line of reasoning

very quickly!" Ryan interrupted him. "Teenagers? Physically healthy people?"

"Senator, if I may . . ."

Ryan cut in again. "Physicians suggesting euthanasia to patients who don't request it? Patients being euthanized without their request? Do you know of even one person who is advocating that we make these activities legal?"

"No I do not, and that is not . . ."

Ryan plowed on again. "Well, then I suggest we deal with reality, with what *is* being proposed!" He was bristling, looking first at a few of his colleagues, then back to Vanzanten.

Vanzanten was unrepentant. "This *is* reality, Senator, and to ignore it and refuse to deal with it is folly."

Ryan glanced over at the TV cameras. Sure enough, most of them had turned in his direction. He shook his head in frustration. "But you just finished telling me that even *you* know of no one who is advocating these activities."

"That's correct and it is precisely the point."

"*What* is precisely the point?"

"That these practices are not what is being advocated today. No one in his right mind would advocate them in North America."

Ryan threw up his hands. "I don't believe this! Then what are you saying?" The room was in a state of silent shock. It had been a long time since any conversation here had elicited this level of passion and intensity.

Vanzanten's eyes flashed as his blood boiled. Enough was enough. The senator's response angered him. This was a challenge not only to his argument but also to his very credibility as a lawyer, and a public challenge at that. Every television camera in the place was now focused on him, awaiting his response, and there was no way he was going to allow some publicity-hungry politician to embarrass him publicly. Leaning forward and ignoring his notes, he took hold of the microphone with both hands. His voice was shrill. "Senator, what you choose to believe is your business."

"Of course it is, but . . ."

"And what I believe," Vanzanten cut in, "is that we must concern ourselves with reality, with the truth, no more and no less."

Ryan glared at him. "What truth?" he shot back.

"The truth about where we are going if we choose to legalize physician-assisted suicide."

"And where is that?"

Vanzanten was still clutching the microphone with both hands. "Virtually everyone realizes that the practices I have mentioned are wrong, in fact tragic, but the truth is that they are where we are heading if we make physician-assisted suicide legal now. That is the kind of society we will most certainly become, and that, Senator, is reality."

Ryan was beginning to calm down. "You mean the slippery slope."

Why slippery slopes exist: because ideas are connected logically

"Yes. Legalizing this practice today will put us on a slippery slope, inviting other practices later such as the ones I have singled out, and probably others as well."

"And this you know how?"

"Because ideas and practices are connected, Senator, and very often one thing leads to another. We even have common expressions used in everyday language showing that we all understand this."

"What common expressions?"

"Give him an inch and he'll take a mile."

"Uh-huh."

Deciding we don't want to move toward other practices does not always prevent the move toward them.

"And we speak of the thin edge of the wedge. It means the same thing. One thing often leads to another, and we know it."

"But why can't we simply decide we don't want to go there?" Ryan persisted. "Why not legalize what we want and not what we don't want? What's the problem?"

"Because it's not that simple."

"Why not?"

"Because moving from physician-assisted suicide to the

other practices I mentioned doesn't happen all at once."

"What do you mean, not all at once?"

"I mean it occurs by a series of very small steps. And while a jump from the first step to the last in any chain of ideas or actions is almost always unthinkable, the move from the first step to the second, and then to the third and so on, is not only possible, sometimes it seems perfectly logical."

How slippery slopes work: in small, logical steps, eventually accepting what was at first unthinkable

This was an idea Ryan would have a tough time speaking against since he had made the same argument himself the previous year during the debate over late-term abortions. While a large number of senators believed in abortion rights, quite a few of them were queasy about late-term abortions, and a bill to ban them had been put forward.

Ryan himself had argued forcefully that prohibiting late-term abortions could lead to a ban on mid-term abortions and eventually on all abortions. "Even in cases of incest and rape!" he had thundered on the senate floor.

Senator Ryan had successfully managed to link one end of the spectrum to the other and to focus people's attention not on the late-term abortions but on the fifteen-year-old victim of incest who could eventually be forced to carry the pregnancy to term if the bill passed. His strategy had worked and the bill had been defeated. *What a great argument,* he had thought to himself at the time.

And he had really believed it, which was why he could speak with such conviction on it. One thing really does lead to another, he had told his colleagues, and patterns and directions are set in motion. This thing had to be nipped in the bud. If the arguments against late-term abortions were accepted, those same arguments could later be marshaled, with only slight revisions, against other abortions too, and he knew it.

And now here the argument was being used again, the identical argument. He had to smile at the irony. And Vanzanten was even using the very terminology Ryan had used the previous year, the thin edge of the wedge. Surely he had not gone back and read Ryan's speech in the senate record and intentionally chosen the expression for that reason. But then again, why not? Ryan knew that if he were in Vanzanten's shoes he would do it. Vanzanten was a lawyer who had students and probably other research assistants at his disposal for this presentation.

Vanzanten was still speaking. "Giving ourselves permission to do one thing often invites the question of permission to do the next thing."

Ryan shook his head in disbelief. These were his very words, lifted right from his speech of the previous year. Did Vanzanten know that, or was this the work of some research assistant who dug them up without Vanzanten's knowledge? Or could it be a coincidence? *God only knows,* Ryan thought to himself. Now he was the one feeling queasy as he saw the knowing smirks of a few of his colleagues whose memories were functioning all too well at the moment.

Sometimes reasons for one action justify other, unintended, actions as well. Vanzanten paused and punched out his next words individually, "But there is more, Senator. Sometimes one action does more than simply *invite* the question of pursuing the next action. There are times when the reasons we set out for doing one thing actually *justify* other actions that we have not yet begun to pursue and may not even be thinking of at the time."

"Thank you for the lesson in logic, Mr. Vanzanten, but can you give this committee some idea of how this might work in an issue like the one we are debating today?"

Vanzanten paused thoughtfully and then replied. "Let me put it to you exactly as one of our physicians recently put it to me." He looked down at his file. "If it makes sense for a physician to heed patient autonomy and leave enough medication with which to commit suicide, does it not also make sense for the same doctor to administer the medication if the patient is incapable of doing so?"

"I suppose so."

"And if it makes sense for the doctor to administer a

lethal dose to someone who is currently requesting it, does it not make sense for the same doctor to give it to someone who only requested it in a will but who is now unconscious?"

The room was quiet, and many people had taken out note pads and were scribbling notes to themselves.

"And if that makes sense," Vanzanten continued, "then does it not make sense to give the lethal injection to a patient who neglected to put it in his will but who frequently spoke of it in positive terms?"

Ryan was following the progression intently, the wheels obviously spinning in his head.

"And if we accept the term *right to die,* knowing that rights imply duties to others, then what about comatose patients who are unable to exercise this right? Are we not depriving them of their rights if we refuse to inject the lethal dose?"

Ryan did not bother to question Vanzanten about this because he had received plenty of mail over the past two months calling on him to honor the so-called right to die.

Vanzanten looked up from the file. "Well of course we are depriving them of their rights," he said dramatically, "if they have this right. And let me add, Senators, that certain euthanasia advocates have already solved this problem for us with their talk of a person's *substituted right to die.* Others have gone farther, speaking of our *duty to die* if we have lived a full life."

Ryan mouthed the words quietly, "Duty to die."

"Do you see, Senator, how quickly we have moved from voluntary euthanasia to involuntary euthanasia? Doing it in one big jump would be too much for anyone, but going one step at a time seems perfectly reasonable, even logical."

The senator wiped his brow with his handkerchief while Vanzanten rearranged his notes and continued. "And there is more reason to think we will slide *down* the slope rather than move up it or even stay at the same place, Senators. There are the *incentives* to move down.

The distinction between incentives and reasons

Incentives to move to other practices

(a) The economic incentive

Not reasons, incentives."

"What are these incentives?"

"The economic incentive, for one."

"Come again?"

"It already exists. The economic incentive that cash-strapped governments everywhere feel to reduce spending. No one knows this better than you, Senator."

This amused Ryan. "I can't argue with that."

"Two important facts must be recognized."

"What are these facts?" Ryan was obviously interested.

"The first is that health-care spending is a large part of most government budgets. That's the easy one."

"True."

"The second is that 30 to 70 percent of all those health-care dollars are spent on people in the last sixty to ninety days of their lives."

"Hmm." This was obviously new to Senator Ryan.

Vanzanten looked up from his legal pad. "Sir, it does not take a lot of figuring to imagine the savings to cash-strapped governments, which are always looking for ways to cut debts and deficits, if even 10 to 20 percent of these people would end their lives before the sixty to ninety days begin. The savings would be dramatic."

Ryan became unhappy. "If you don't mind me saying so, Mr. Vanzanten, something tells me you have a low opinion of the citizens of this country. I don't."

What political claptrap! Vanzanten felt like shouting. *Blatant political nonsense.* "Nothing could be further from the truth, Senator," he said instead. "And with all due respect, it's quite clear that you've missed the point."

"I've missed the point, have I?" Ryan leaned forward. "Then you tell me, are you not implying that the people of this country would be willing to euthanize more and more older people to save money? Isn't that your point, sir? Just how many citizens do you think would ever argue that we should do that?"

"Virtually no one."

Ryan threw up his hands again. "Mr. Vanzanten, are

you trying to be confusing here? Because if you are, you're succeeding."

"No, sir, I'm not. My point is really a very simple one. It is that although very few people will ever explicitly argue that we should euthanize older people or anyone else, there will be an economic incentive, usually subconscious, moving us all in that direction. It is one that none of us will be able to ignore. It will be in the back of our thinking at all times because it is reality."

The wheels were spinning in Ryan's mind as he mulled over the significance of this economic incentive.

Vanzanten spoke again. "I implore you, senators, not to deny that this incentive will exist. If we do so we are putting our heads in the sand. The incentive will be there, and it will apply pressure on us to slide down the slope, to have *more* euthanasia rather then less because more euthanasia will lead to dramatically reduced medical costs."

There was silence for a few seconds, and Ryan finished writing. Then he looked over the top of his reading glasses. "For the record," he said, "do you see any other incentives that could move us down the slippery slope?"

"There is one other," Vanzanten replied, "and I'm afraid it is one that some people here today will understand all too well. They know it and feel it."

"It sounds serious. What is it?"

"The family incentive."

"The family incentive? I'm afraid I don't follow."

(b) The family incentive

"If you have ever gone through the pain of seeing a loved one suffer from a terminal illness, or a long-term debilitating disease or a serious accident, you know that care-giving family members experience grave burdens and inconveniences."

"Yes, I know that to be true," replied Ryan, cooling down from the previous few exchanges.

"Caring for dependent loved ones in the home requires incredible time and energy and is a constant emotional drain. It means endless visits to the hospital, doctor's office, pharmacy and so on. It might mean bathing and toileting the loved one."

Senators across the front were nodding their agreement.

Vanzanten's voice quieted and grew intense as he continued. "Senators, if you have been there you know that even the most saintly person in that situation cannot be blamed for having the occasional thought that it would be nice if it were over."[2]

"Aren't you being a little hard on these caregivers, Mr. Vanzanten?"

"Just the opposite, Senator."

Ryan shifted his position uncomfortably.

"These people are selfless. They make the world a better place. And the work they do is often thankless and done quietly, without fanfare. We owe a debt of gratitude to every one of them for the wonderful service they provide to the weakest members of our society. But who could blame them for occasionally wishing the burden could be lifted? Would you blame them, Senator, for occasionally wishing that?"

"OK, I see your point."

Vanzanten closed his file, leaned forward and clutched the microphone. "Let us remember, Senators, that these subconscious incentives, both economic and family, are on the side of moving down the slope, not up, making it even more likely that that will be the direction in which we move."

An aide leaned forward and whispered in Senator Ryan's ear. "It is time for a short recess," Ryan said. "Ten minutes." With a rap of the gavel he brought the session to a close. Immediately the room was filled with the sound of chairs moving and people talking.

Ron watched as once again the TV cameras and a flood of reporters rushed over to Senator Ryan, who gushed about how productive the hearings had become and how important they were for honoring the liberties and rights of the citizens whom he was elected to serve. He made sure they knew how strongly he felt that the people must be given a voice on issues like this one.

A few reporters were also asking Vanzanten to clarify his distinction between arguments and incentives. Ron headed out the door. The lines to the water fountains looked like they would never end.

13

S enator Ryan cleared his throat and looked up from what he had been writing. He was visibly irritated with Vanzanten, whose part of the presentation he had hoped would be over when the hearings resumed. It wasn't. Ryan called the audience to order and began by addressing the attorney. "Frankly, Mr. Vanzanten, you are not the first one to mention this slippery slope this week."

"I know that."

"And others believe we can carefully craft the law in such a way as to prevent this slide down the slope, as you call it."

Vanzanten was quick to respond. "And as a lawyer yourself, Senator, you know that the fact that certain people do or do not believe something makes it neither true nor false."

Ryan glared at him. He did not appreciate the lecture.

"An idea or argument," Vanzanten continued, "must be judged on its own merits, and on this issue the slippery slope is no joke. To ignore it is to put our heads in the sand. We do that at our own peril."

Is the slippery slope inevitable? The senator rubbed his forehead. "And you would have us believe that the slide down this slippery slope is inevitable, unstoppable? Is that your contention?"

"Yes."

"Do you have a crystal ball, sir?"

Vanzanten laughed loudly, looking over at Buckley.

Ryan scowled contemptuously at him. "Is this funny,

Mr. Vanzanten?" He had long since given up on all efforts to hide his dislike for the lawyer.

"Only your question, Senator. The issue itself is a matter of life and death. Since you ask, of course I have no crystal ball."

"Then how can you make such an assertion about the future? How could anyone? Aren't you being just a little overconfident, sir, in telling us this slippery slope will be unstoppable?"

Vanzanten took a quick sip of water. "It's a strong term, I admit, and it should be used with great care," he said. "But with all due respect, we don't need a crystal ball to see that once we begin on this path, future movement down the slippery slope will be impossible to stop."

"And this you know how?" The senator punched out each word loudly and dramatically.

The room grew eerily quiet as many wondered if Vanzanten had bitten off more than he could chew. After all, these senators were lawyers, educators and professionals themselves. It wouldn't be easy to pull the wool over their eyes.

Vanzanten turned a page in his file and began to speak. *A slippery slope demonstrated by recent experience* "In 1991 a fifty-year-old woman in the Netherlands who was physically healthy but seriously depressed sought a physician-assisted suicide from her psychiatrist and received one."

"Do you have documentation on that?"

"*Time* magazine wrote up the story, and it's very easily verified."[1]

Ryan paused, then cupped his hand over his microphone and leaned back to whisper something to an aide, who immediately scurried out of the room.

"Was this legal in the Netherlands at the time?"

"No it was not, and that is precisely the point."

"*What* is precisely the point?"

Vanzanten took another drink of water and thought about how to respond. "Let me put it this way, Senator. This case clearly demonstrates what happens to a public policy that is based on the right of a woman to choose to end her life with the aid of a physician when she decides her suffering is too great and does not want to endure it any longer."

"Yes, and what happens to policies like these?"

"In this case, the physician went to court for his illegal activity and was exonerated."

"How could he be exonerated? It was against the law."

Vanzanten smiled. "Perhaps the better question is, How could he have been convicted?"

This intrigued Ryan. "What do you mean?"

"I mean this woman was suffering grievously," Vanzanten replied. "She had an abusive, alcoholic husband and two sons. Both sons died, one through suicide."

Ryan grimaced.

"And the woman had decided that her suffering was too great and that she did not want to endure it any longer, just as the advocates of euthanasia say. So she asked for a physician-assisted suicide and got it. Why wouldn't she? The only difference was that her suffering was psychological, not physical."

"Which is an important difference, is it not, Mr. Vanzanten?"

Is there an important difference between intolerable *physical* suffering and intolerable *psychological* suffering? "You and I may think so, but her doctor and her lawyer didn't. In fact, her lawyer's very words after the verdict were that the court decision showed that intolerable psychological suffering was no different than intolerable physical suffering."

Then Vanzanten looked directly at the senator. "I think he had a point, Senator. Don't you? Most people who become suicidal are that way because of psychological or emotional suffering, not physical."

Ryan was not convinced. "But that was not the intent of the law! That's the difference!"

"Exactly!"

"What?"

"I said exactly! That is precisely the point."

The senator leaned back and squinted at Vanzanten

over the top of his glasses, waiting for him to continue.

"The Dutch law was originally intended for a few exceptional cases of people with terminal illnesses who are in the dying phase of life," Vanzanten explained. "It was not intended for people whose suffering was only psychological, but that is where it went because the principle on which the law is based was being interpreted consistently. Remember what that principle says. The person suffering is the one who decides when the suffering is too great and that they want to end it with a physician's help. That is the whole point of making physician-assisted suicide legal—to give the suffering person that choice." *The PAS principle justifies much more than advocates of PAS intend.*

Ryan leaned forward close to the microphone. "Let me get this straight. This physician violated the safeguards, and according to you there was no way to stop him?"

"That is correct. Let's be clear on exactly what happened in this case. The Dutch safeguards that were intended precisely to prevent the move down the slippery slope to other unwanted practices could not stop that slide, because the law making physician-assisted suicide legal rests on the principle that the individual has the right to choose. That is always the most fundamental reason given for why the practice ought to be legalized." *Third argument opposing PAS: the impotence of safeguards*

"Uh-huh."

"The problem is that the safeguards conflicted with the fundamental principle of personal autonomy, and so they, the safeguards, were struck down and rewritten. The courts in the Netherlands simply did what courts do."

"I think I understand courts, Mr. Vanzanten."

"Then you know that they apply principles and legal precedents consistently, and in the Netherlands the result has been that the law making physician-assisted suicide legal has been broadened repeatedly by court rulings just like this one. Euthanasia has been made easier and available to more people than was ever intended in the beginning."[2]

By this time Ryan's aide was back and again leaning forward to whisper in his ear. The senator asked, "How have the safeguards changed, Mr. Vanzanten?"

Vanzanten quickly pulled another file from a document case beside him. He opened the file, and his eyes quickly landed on the desired document. "In 1973," he began, "when the first court opinion suggested guidelines, a patient was required to have an incurable condition, to be experiencing unbearable suffering, to have put the request for physician-assisted suicide in writing and to have begun the dying phase."

"That was 1973?" Ryan asked, making notes to himself.

"Yes. Some time later the Dutch Medical Association developed its own guidelines to help clarify matters for physicians. Notice the changes in their guidelines. According to the new guidelines, the patient no longer was required to have begun the dying phase. Furthermore, a request in writing was no longer required; instead, written documentation was now merely said to be helpful."

"Helpful," Ryan muttered to himself.

The most important safeguard and the problem with it "I should add," Vanzanten said, looking directly at the row of senators, "that the safeguard requiring a written request is the most important one for the patient, and it is recommended by virtually all advocates of euthanasia. Unfortunately it will always be the first one to be struck down."

"Why is that?" queried the senator.

"Because it will immediately be seen to be discriminatory against those patients who are too weak or debilitated to write."

"Hmm." This was obviously a new idea to Ryan. "So the most important safeguard will be the first to go."

"Correct, as it was in the Netherlands."

Murmuring and mumbling could be heard across the room.

"There's more," Vanzanten continued. "In 1986 safeguards were eroded further when the high court of The Hague, the final court of appeal, declared that the dire distress of a nonterminal patient in the advanced stages of multiple sclerosis may justify euthanasia. In other words, not only was it no longer required that the patient be in the dying phase, the illness need not even be terminal."

"Uh-huh."

"Soon after that the Advocate General at the Court of Justice in the Hague summed up the Netherlands' situation by saying that the safe terrain, as he called it, of *physical* suffering, which can almost always be demonstrated, had been abandoned. Now, he said, they were in a murky area—his word—in which unbearable *psychological* feelings of displeasure are used to determine whether to perform euthanasia. This is the slope traveled in the Netherlands."

Ryan put down his pen and pulled off his glasses. "Are you convinced that we would travel this road too?"

Vanzanten closed his file and wiped his forehead. "Senator, what I am about to say now is the most important part of my presentation today." All of the senators across the front looked up. Ron leaned forward, craning his neck to look past people who were blocking his view of Vanzanten.

Senator Ryan looked back and forth at his colleagues then nodded at Vanzanten. "We have our pens ready, Mr. Vanzanten."

"I would draw your attention to something I said earlier."

"Yes?"

"That sometimes the reasons we give for doing one thing unwittingly justify other things that we are not thinking of at the time."

"Yes, you said that before."

"Bear with me one more time on this. Notice exactly what the principle states on which physician-assisted suicide is based."

"Yes."

"It declares that any person who decides her suffering is too great has the right to request and receive a physician-assisted suicide."

The secret of the slippery slope: Reasons for one action sometimes also justify other unintended actions.

"Uh-huh. I can see we're all going to know that principle very well by the time you're finished with us."

Critical question: If PAS is legalized, will there be a basis for denying unintended requests for PAS? "I trust so. And the question that Physicians for Compassionate Care wishes to leave with you today is this. If we put this principle into law, how can we deny a physician-assisted suicide to a twenty-five-year-old anorexic woman who requests it, just as one did in the Netherlands not long ago? She received it. How could we deny a similar request?"

Ryan shrugged and shook his head.

"Or the request of the fifty-year-old, depressed woman I spoke of earlier?"

Ryan wanted to disagree but wasn't sure how to at the moment.

Then Vanzanten leaned forward and zeroed in on the row of senators. "How, I ask you, could we even deny it to a teenager who is physically healthy but deeply depressed and wants to end his suffering with an assisted suicide?"

This one touched a raw nerve, Vanzanten could tell. Ryan's face reddened. He wanted to shout that we are not talking about teenagers, that this right to an assisted suicide is not intended for them, but he knew Vanzanten would take his statement and milk it for all it was worth. Of course it's not, Vanzenten would shout back, and then he would challenge Ryan to show him how he would stop it from spreading to teenagers who were suffering and wanted to die. There was no use providing him more fuel for the fire.

Vanzanten continued, sounding more like a crusader all the time, "The principle says that it is he, the one suffering, who is to decide whether or not his suffering is too great and that he wants an assisted suicide. Not us. That is the point of the principle of autonomy. The right to choose for oneself. It is the fundamental argument of all euthanasia advocates."

Camera crews were pointing at Vanzanten and moving in closer as he continued, his voice rising.

"What will we tell this teenager? That his suffering is

not bad enough? How could we know that? What arrogance on our part to tell him that! Or will we tell him that his suffering is the wrong kind of suffering? On what basis would we say that? Or will we say that physician-assisted suicide was not intended for him? What does he care?" Vanzanten declared, pausing dramatically to leave his questions ringing in the ears of everyone in the room.

Ryan sat stone-faced.

Vanzanten continued. "You and I may say all those things and really believe them. But the courts won't because they will do what courts do. They are in the business of interpreting principles and precedents consistently. Reasons for the original principle unwittingly become reasons for granting an assisted suicide to people far beyond those it was originally intended for."

Ryan again rubbed his forehead. "I have to admit, Mr. Vanzanten, you make an interesting case."

Vanzanten nodded his thanks. For a moment it looked as if a mutual, professional respect might be developing between the senator and the lawyer.

"I want to conclude this section of our presentation by telling you that in the Netherlands today about half of Dutch doctors feel it is legitimate to suggest to patients that they consider euthanasia. I ask you to imagine being sick, weak, possibly elderly, and being told by your doctor that you might consider euthanasia. That type of suggestion is commonplace in Dutch hospitals, and it compromises the voluntariness of euthanasia."

Ryan leaned forward. "Just before you conclude . . . for the record, didn't you say something earlier about people in the Netherlands being euthanized with no request?"

"Yes, I did."

"That is a serious charge. Would you care to expand on it?"

"Yes, I would. It is documented in a study done by the Dutch government itself," he replied without looking down at his notes, "which points out that over one thousand patients each year in the Netherlands are euthanized with no request. This figure is undisputed, Senator."[3]

The senator shook his head and wrote something down.

"It should be clear," said Vanzanten, "that in the Netherlands what was initially intended for a few exceptional cases, just as the advocates of euthanasia are now arguing that it should be here, has become accepted and routine. Why should we think we are better than the Dutch?"

Vanzanten's presentation was finished. He closed his file and leaned back, waiting for a signal from the senator on what was happening next. The senator had cupped his hand over the microphone again and was whispering to the aide behind him as well as the senators on either side. He looked at his watch, nodded at his colleagues while mouthing something to them, then leaned forward to the microphone.

"Dr. Buckley and Mr. Vanzanten, you've been provocative here today."

"We're actually very nice people," Buckley joked.

Ryan smiled and looked at her over his reading glasses. "I'm sure that's true, Doctor. In any case, a number of my colleagues would like to question you further about some things you both have said. I've decided to invite you to return after our lunch recess to entertain those questions."

Ryan's gavel fell. "This hearing stands in recess until one o'clock."

14

Ron made a beeline for the hallway and headed toward the building's entrance, where he saw that a group of taxis had pulled up. "What a life," he muttered, running down the huge corridor and through the main doors and climbing into the back seat of a taxi, which quickly pulled out into the busy traffic.

As he rode, Ron stared blankly out the window. Men and women in business suits talked on their cellular phones as they walked purposefully down the sidewalk. A short distance away a group of young mothers pushed their babies in strollers, talking and laughing to one another.

Ron wondered how many of these people cared about the issue that had consumed him for the past two weeks until he could think of little else. How many even knew the hearings were underway? *They're probably just like I was a month ago,* he thought, *until Patrick called.*

Suddenly the taxi jerked to a stop. Ron paid the cab fare and headed toward a small pub where a lunch crowd was gathering outside. *The food must be OK,* he thought, *with all these people coming in.* After he took a seat, he studied the menu and watched as harried servers rushed frantically between customers, the food-preparation area and the bar.

Eventually a server noticed him and hurried over. She was young and bright, and appeared to be handling the lunch hour bedlam with more grace and humor than most of her coworkers. Ron had already heard one exasperated server losing his patience with a patron over the exact blend of the man's drink. The server had finally shaken his head and gone for a replacement.

"Good afternoon, sir," the waitress said cheerfully, above the din. "Welcome to our quiet little getaway."

Ron liked her. She had spunk and good humor in the midst of chaos. "I'll have a chicken Caesar salad with a martini, please," he said with a laugh.

"Coming right up," she replied, and she was gone as quickly as she had come. Ron looked around the room, spotted a pay phone in the far corner and walked over to it. After Judy's news about the ATN calls last night, he wanted to be kept informed of any new media calls. He pushed his coins in, dialed the Hilton and asked for messages.

There were two, the woman at the front desk told him. Both were from reporters, one from a Julia Benthall at ATN and the other from a Scott Becker with the local *Springfield Sun*. Both callers were asking him to call at his earliest convenience. She gave him their phone numbers.

"Are there any other messages?" Ron asked, disappointed at his take.

"That's all, Dr. Grey."

Ron stared at the piece of paper with the names and numbers as he walked slowly back to his table. A thousand questions swirled through his mind, not the least of which was how they had gotten his number in the first place. How did they know where he was staying? How much else did they already know? What kind of story did they have in mind? Was there any way to stop them from using his name? What would he say if he were asked a question he didn't want to answer? Would they ask him questions they already knew the answers to just to see if he was answering honestly? Was that how these people operated? He didn't know. What he did know was that he would be in over his head dealing with reporters, who are trained to investigate and get information out of people. If they caught him trying to mislead them, would that be included in their story? He quickly decided that any kind of dishonesty was out of the question.

Settling in his chair, Ron looked at the ceiling and thought hard about these questions. He finally decided on a safe and simple strategy. The server returned with his order, and he began picking at the chicken in his salad. He would have nothing to say to Julia Benthall. He would call Scott Becker after lunch.

Ron stirred his Caesar salad and picked at it some more. It had been nicely prepared and was surprisingly tasty, but thoughts of talking to Scott Becker were working havoc on his enjoyment of it. Glancing at his watch, he pushed aside the rest of the salad and strode to the pay phone. The background din of the full restaurant provided a cover of privacy as he entered the number of Scott Becker at the *Springfield Sun.*

A very businesslike receptionist answered and immediately put him through. Becker picked up his phone. "Scott Becker." His voice was deep and loud, and he sounded rushed and harried.

"This is Ron Grey," Ron replied, holding the phone two inches from his ear.

"Yes, Dr. Grey," Becker gushed, immediately friendly and no longer in a rush. "Thank you for calling. Let me get right to the point. We have tracked down a rumor that you may be the physician Dr. Patrick Metcalfe has asked to administer a physician-assisted suicide to him. Can you either confirm or deny this rumor?"

"No."

"Well, uh, that is the rumor we've heard."

"Where did you hear it?"

"Well, you know, we have sources and we need to protect their privacy. I can't really tell you where we heard it. Would you like to comment on this rumor?"

"Not over the phone."

"Are you a friend of Dr. Metcalfe?"

"Sure."

"Could we meet?"

Ron's mind raced. Why would he want to meet with this reporter and give him more information when what he really wanted was for the story to go away? On the other hand, if he talked directly to Becker, maybe he could have some control over the story. He could make sure they at least got their facts correct. "Yes I can," he replied, "privately, for a few minutes, later today."

"Great. There's a Green Country Inn on Volley Street, two blocks from the senate building," Becker said. "How about 4:30? You'll be done at the hearings by then."

Ron rolled his eyes. "How'd you know I was at the hearings?"

Becker laughed for the first time. "That kind of information is for sale, if you know what I mean."

Ron wondered what else he already knew from his sources and would be looking for Ron to confirm.

"There's a quiet, dark lounge called the Evergreen in the back of the Green Country Inn," Becker explained. "We'll meet there."

"Come alone," Ron directed. "Just you and me, OK?"

"Of course."

Ron hung the phone up, glanced at his watch and rushed out to grab a taxi. *Great,* he thought. *I'll be late for the hearings.*

15

As Ron walked softly into the hearings chamber, the room was quiet and Ryan was introducing another senator who would be the first to question Buckley and Vanzanten. Senator Barbara Longfellow was highly articulate and oozed confidence. She appeared to be very adept at the art of dialogue and was almost intimidating.

Senator Longfellow leaned forward with her hands folded on the massive desk in front of her and looked at Vanzanten and Buckley, saying nothing for a few seconds. Then she smiled and spoke. "I'd like to get at something very basic," she began.

Vanzanten and Buckley nodded.

"And that is that regardless of the reasons you or anyone else believes this practice should not be legalized, isn't it really an issue of personal choice, individual liberty?"

"That's one issue," Buckley responded.

"I think it's *the* issue," Senator Longfellow said, removing her glasses and looking intently into Buckley's eyes. "As we sit here today debating, people out there," she waved her hand toward the open windows, "are suffering and want to end their suffering gently and peacefully."

"Yes, that's true," Buckley acknowledged.

"In my opinion," Senator Longfellow continued, "the right to avoid suffering and pain is basic. It's fundamental. What right do you or anyone else have to ignore their wishes, to deny them this liberty? After all, the only thing they are asking for is to end their own suffering in a gentle and painless way. Who are we to force them to go on suf-

Fourth argument opposing PAS: The right to individual autonomy does not require the legalization of PAS.

fering when they do not wish to?"

Buckley leaned into her microphone, about to respond, but the senator quite obviously was not finished. Buckley cleared her throat and sat back again.

"Let me paint a picture for you," Longfellow continued. "I think it will demonstrate what I mean."

Buckley and Vanzanten looked at each other and shrugged. Why not?

"Suppose one of you," the senator said, pointing directly at Buckley and Vanzanten, "met someone who was suffering intensely and who wanted to end the suffering."

She paused to let that thought sink in.

"Do you think," she continued, leaning forward and looking at them carefully, "that you would have the right to make that person go on suffering?" Longfellow knew that many in the audience had been persuaded by both Buckley's and Vanzanten's presentations. Sitting back, she also realized that by simply asking her question this way, she would cause many of them to reconsider. It was a good question and she knew it.

Buckley leaned forward and folded her hands. "Senator, I have never argued that there are not some people who want the right to receive a physician-assisted suicide. Clearly, some do."

Longfellow threw up her hands. "My point exactly!"

"But," continued Buckley, "I have to tell you that I am surprised at how often advocates of euthanasia tell us exactly this."

"Exactly what?"

(a) Examining the right to individual autonomy "What you told us just now, that there are people who want the choice to use the medical profession to help end their lives, as though somehow the fact that somebody *wants* to do something is sufficient reason for making it a legal and free activity."[1]

"Dr. Buckley," Senator Longfellow cut in, "nothing is more important than the liberty of our citizens. Frankly, people like you frighten me."

What a crock! Vanzanten felt like shouting. *What blatant scare tactics.*

Longfellow continued. "People like you are all too ready to enact new laws and prohibitions against the things you disagree with. Every law is a restriction on our liberty. Laws curtail liberty. They restrain it. Let us never forget that. I, for one, think we have too many laws in this country already!"

"More political grandstanding," Vanzanten muttered, looking down at the table.

Buckley took a sip of water. "I assume you're a libertarian," she said to Senator Longfellow, switching into her political mode, something she had grown accustomed to doing through her media experiences.

"Yes I am. I value individual liberty greatly. I suppose you have a problem with that?"

"No, as a matter of fact, I don't. I'm especially glad that you, Senator, in your position, value individual liberty so highly. But as a lawmaker you also know that it is never enough, even for a libertarian, to simply ask whether a person *wants* to do something when deciding whether or not to make an activity legal. Many people want to do many things. Some of those things are very good, some are very bad, and of course there is a whole range in between." (b) A person's *desire* to perform an action is never by itself an adequate reason to legalize the action.

"True enough," Longfellow shrugged.

"And would you seriously suggest that we give anyone and everyone complete liberty to perform any activity just so long as they *want* to perform it? What about the person who enjoys drinking and driving? What of the person who wants to steal from elderly people? These people *want* to do these things."

The doctor sat back and waited for a response from the senator, who grabbed her own microphone. "But these actions are different! You know that! To compare actions like these with physician-assisted suicide is preposterous! They shouldn't even be used in the same sentence!"

Buckley quickly leaned forward again. "And would you

mind telling me just how they are different?"

"They are harmful to other people! That's how! Drinking and driving harms people! Stealing violates the people stolen from! Can't you see that?" The senator's voice had risen to a high pitch. "That is why we make them illegal!"

This was exactly the answer Dr. Buckley had been anticipating. "Let me get this straight, Senator Longfellow. Are you, a libertarian, telling us that it is good and right to place legal restrictions on people, to stop them from doing things they want to do just so long as the actions they want to perform would be harmful to others? Is that what you just said, Senator?"

"Yes, and that's the only reason we should restrict people—harm to others."

Buckley laughed aloud. "I couldn't have said it better myself."

Senator Longfellow was not laughing. "You couldn't have said *what* better yourself, Doctor?"

"That the reason we ought to make certain activities illegal is because they harm others. It's the reason we have laws against all sorts of things people would *like* to do. We have zoning laws, traffic laws, laws against breaking and entering."

The senator listened, almost incredulously. She should be the one saying these things, she thought.

The doctor continued. "Every one of these laws stops people from doing things they want to do. In fact, our prisons are filled with people who have wanted to do certain activities so badly that they went ahead anyway, in spite of the restrictions against them."

Longfellow looked defiant. "Would you mind telling me what this has to do with physician-assisted suicide? Surely you're not telling us that it causes harm to others."

Buckley quickly leaned into her microphone. "That is exactly what I'm telling you, Senator."

(c) PAS is not a purely private act. "C'mon, Doctor! Physician-assisted suicide is a private act that would be carried out by a few suffering people who simply want to end their suffering. It causes no harm to others."

Buckley leaned over and whispered something to Van-zanten, who listened and whispered something back. Then she spoke softly into the microphone. "With the greatest of respect, Senator, nothing could be further from the truth. In fact, that is a misrepresentation of what is really at stake."

"A misrepresentation?"

"Yes."

This irked Longfellow. She looked at her notes and then back up at Buckley. "Where is the misrepresentation?"

"It's a misrepresentation to present this issue as merely a matter of an individual's choice to end suffering, with no effects on anyone else."

Longfellow was dissatisfied with the answer. "How so?"

"Because it is more than just a private action. It is a public policy change."

A few senators nodded, making note of the difference on their legal pads.

"And whenever we change public policy, we must show that the new policy will bring about more good than harm to the people directly affected by it. Is that not true, Senator?"

Longfellow shrugged again and nodded.

"Of course," Buckley continued, "that means we must analyze the effects of the new policy." (d) New public policies must be evaluated for their effects on people.

"Uh-huh."

"To simply appeal to individual choice, or liberty or autonomy as *the reason* for implementing any new public policy, including this one, is grossly inadequate. In fact, I find it quite irresponsible."

This was an argument Buckley had used over and over again in the media. And it usually resonated with audiences. Most people quickly understood that, however appealing individual liberty and autonomy sounded at first, the simple fact that some person *wanted* to do something was never enough reason for making the desired activity legal. Furthermore, no one wants to be seen as irresponsible, and it seemed only reasonable to ask people to consider the consequences of a new public policy before implementing it. It was an argument that worked and Buckley was glad for a chance to use it here.

"So the question that we ought to be asking," Dr. Buckley continued, "is what the effects will be of changing this public policy in order to give people the right to use the medical profession to help end their lives. If the effects are good, then let's get on with it, legalize physician-assisted suicide and put the issue behind us. But if the effects are bad and harmful to people, let's reject physician-assisted suicide as bad public policy and come up with a new, different policy that will better serve our neediest and most vulnerable citizens."

"Vulnerable citizens? Who do you mean?"

(e) Legalizing PAS harms vulnerable people.

"The elderly, the terminally ill, even the disabled. These classes of people will all be affected by any change in this public policy, and it should be obvious that they are our most vulnerable citizens."

"And how will they be affected? Are you seriously telling us that legalizing physician-assisted suicide would be harmful to these vulnerable citizens?" It was clear that this was a new concept to the senator.

"Yes I am."

"How?" she asked again.

"By imposing a severe burden on these entire classes of people."

"What burden?"

"To put it bluntly, Senator, it would put them in the position of having to justify their own continued existence, and this at the weakest, most vulnerable time in their lives."

Buckley's words caught Ron's attention. This was the same point Dr. Grange had made the day before at the palliative-care ward at Southside Medical. It was an idea that had weighed heavily on his mind during the night when he should have been sleeping. Grange's little mental exercise had been more effective than Ron had wished.

Ron couldn't stop thinking about what it must be like to be dependent upon others for everything, to know that you are burden and an expense to others and to wish that you weren't such a burden. The part that really stuck in Ron's mind, however, had not even been mentioned by Grange. It had to do with the family members and loved ones left behind when the person ended her life. He knew how awful the parents of suicide victims felt, how they grieved and mourned and wondered if it had happened because of something they had said or done, or had failed to say or do. *The special grief experienced by people whose loved ones commit suicide: "Was it because of me? If only I had ..."*

How much different could it be for the *children* of people who committed suicide? How could they, the children, avoid asking the same questions, at least in some cases? Did my loved one end her life because she saw what a burden she was to me and my family? Did she see the strain and pressure in my eyes? Should I have hidden that look of strain from her? Was I guilty of somehow allowing her to feel she was a burden? How could the children not wonder about questions like these? *Might the loved ones of PAS "victims" wonder about the same questions?*

Ron looked up to see Buckley opening another file as she continued to speak. She had obviously finished answering Senator Longfellow's question, but before Ryan could move to another senator's question, Buckley was telling him she had one more thing to say about the matter of individual liberty, or personal autonomy as they were calling it.

"Go ahead," Senator Ryan said, glancing at his watch. "But please be brief."

"It seems to me," Dr. Buckley began, looking directly at Longfellow again, "that your main argument for legalizing physician-assisted suicide is that individual autonomy requires it."

"Yes, that's right," answered Longfellow. "There should be a basic right to choose to end one's suffering in a gentle and humane way. It's nothing more than respecting people's individual liberty."

"And I have tried to show," Buckley continued, "that the simple fact that people want to do certain things is never enough reason to legalize something. We must at least ask whether the actions in question will harm others."

"Yes, you've argued that."

"But I'm willing to forget all about that argument for a moment," Buckley said. "Ignore it, because I have a different question for you, if you don't mind."

"Not at all." Longfellow appeared eager to engage the doctor in dialogue once again.

"Do you really believe," Buckley asked, "that legalizing physician-assisted suicide will actually increase personal autonomy for suffering people?"

Fifth argument opposing PAS: Individual autonomy is not enhanced by legalizing PAS.

The senator jerked backward, shook her head, then looked back and forth at her colleagues. Raising her hands, she asked, "Am I missing something here, Doctor? Of course it would. How could it not increase liberty? If this service were legal and available, people would then be free to do something that they cannot now do. Where I come from, that is an increase in liberty."

Buckley nodded and paused. "A few minutes ago, you asked me if I believed I had the right to force someone to go on suffering when they no longer wanted to."

"I certainly did," Longfellow replied, "and frankly I'm surprised you would raise my question again. I thought you might want to avoid it."

"Not at all. I love that question," Buckley smiled. "I've raised it again because I'd like to give you the same opportunity you gave me to answer it."

Longfellow was mystified. "You're kidding, right?"

"I've never been more serious, Senator."

Senator Longfellow shook her head again. "Well then, of course I have no right to force a suffering person to go on suffering when that person would rather die. That's my answer. Suffering people should have the right to choose to end their lives gently and peacefully. That's the whole point of legalizing this practice."

Buckley eyed Longfellow very carefully and paused again. The room grew quiet as people strained their necks to look at Buckley. Longfellow watched her and waited. Buckley paused longer. Finally Senator Ryan spoke. "Dr. Buckley, do you wish to respond?"

"Yes, I do," she answered firmly. Speaking very softly, she looked directly at Longfellow. "What if the person is not elderly or ill at all but rather is a middle-aged person who is physically healthy but seriously depressed?" Buckley spoke louder, "No, let me go further. What if the suffering person is a teenage boy, as we spoke of earlier, who is physically healthy but whose life has been hell? Family breakup, abuse, failure in school. The teenager is a loner. What if *this* suffering person came to you, Senator, and said, 'My suffering is too great. I don't want to endure it any longer. I want a physician-assisted suicide.' Would you, Senator, grant him this wish, or would you force him, as you put it, to go on enduring his suffering?"

Longfellow exploded. "No! A thousand times no! I would not grant a person like this an assisted suicide. He has so much to live for."

This was too much for Buckley. "But didn't you just say," she thundered back, "that the reason we ought to legalize physician-assisted suicide is so that suffering people who no longer want to endure their suffering can choose," she paused after this word, and then repeated it, "*choose* to end their suffering with the help of a physician? If I'm not mistaken, those were your words, Senator!"

"But the service would not be intended for people like that!" the senator fired back.

"Now that is very interesting!" Buckley exclaimed. "And who decides who it is intended for?"

"The lawmakers of this state," Senator Longfellow responded, "the same people who would legalize the practice in the first place, and people in the medical community, of course. We would have safeguards in place to deter-

The decision to die is made by others, not the patient, if PAS is legalized.

mine exactly who could and could not receive the service."

"Exactly!" exclaimed Buckley.

"What?" Longfellow raised her hands in frustration.

"I said, 'Exactly!' In other words," Buckley continued, "the suffering person himself does not, in the end, make the choice of whether or not he will receive a physician-assisted suicide, does he, Senator? All he can do is ask for one. Someone else will decide if he actually gets one."

"What are you saying, Doctor?"

"I'm saying that by your own account, Senator, the final choice about who will and will not receive a physician-assisted suicide is not that of the suffering person at all is it? It is the legal and medical communities that make the safeguards. You just said it. So where's the autonomy for the patient?"

Dr. Buckley's voice was rising as she went on. "In our view, this is incredibly serious. Not only would legalizing this practice impose a devastating burden on vulnerable people and open the way for other abuses by removing the pillars of protection for them—the present laws that prohibit anyone from helping another person die. But it would also do all of this without even achieving the very goal it sets out to achieve: patient autonomy. This is incoherent, Senator, and we're messing around with the protection of our most vulnerable people."[2]

Senator Longfellow felt like she had been backed into a corner and was livid. "But there are always limits on individual liberty. We have the liberty to drive automobiles, but that doesn't mean that any person can drive any car, any place, at any speed or in any lane. If you want to drive, you have to earn a license to drive, and the conditions for that are set by the government. Even after that you have to drive according to limits and laws that are also established by the government. All of these conditions are placed on drivers, but none of them destroys the liberty we have to drive cars."

"True," Buckley replied. "But your analogy breaks down because once you pass the driving test and agree to drive within the law, *you* are the one who makes the decision to go for a drive. If you want go, you go. If you don't, you stay home. But this is *not* the case with physician-assisted suicide. If it is legalized and you or I ask for one, others will still decide whether or not we receive it. All the suffering person can do is put in his request and wait to have his fate decided by someone else."

Longfellow was just about to respond, but Senator Ryan spoke first. "I think you've both made your points. We have other senators with questions and one more delegation waiting to make a presentation.

Longfellow glared at Ryan first and then at Buckley, obviously unhappy that she was not given the last word, then slumped back in her chair. Buckley looked back at her and then over to Ryan who was introducing the next senator. His name was Murray Goethe, a huge bearded man who looked like he belonged on a football field rather than in the senate.

Ron had begun to enjoy and look forward to the exchanges between the senators and the delegates. It was stimulating, sometimes tense and always helpful. It was an opportunity to dig deeper into key questions that he wondered about. As he looked at Senator Goethe, Ron wondered what questions would be on his mind.

Argument from analogy must be similar at relevant points. In this case, who makes the final decision?

16

Ryan had just given Senator Goethe the floor. The huge man leaned forward, pausing dramatically as he looked at Vanzanten and Buckley. Then he blurted out the words, "But aren't they happening anyway?"

Vanzanten and Buckley looked blankly at one another, shrugged and shook their heads. "You'll have to help us out a little here," Dr. Buckley said.

"Assisted suicides!" he blurted again. "Aren't they going on anyway . . . whether you like it or not?"

Suddenly Buckley knew exactly where the senator was going with this question. "Uh-huh," she replied, reaching for her microphone to respond further. Goethe, however, was not finished and immediately spoke again, leaving no time for responses just yet.

Assisted suicides happen even if illegal, sometimes with horrific results. "We had a delegation here on Monday," he elaborated, "that told us that assisted suicides are happening now— friends helping friends die, and not always with happy results, I might add. In fact, some of these are botched, with miserable results. This delegation even left us a published work detailing some of these botched attempts," he said, wildly waving the book left by the delegation so all could see.

"We are aware of this work," Buckley interjected. "Perhaps you could tell us precisely what your point is about these botched suicides?" She knew full well what the argument was, having encountered it often on radio call-in programs. In fact, a prepared response lay next to her in a file. But she wanted the senator to clarify the argument on his own. There was no point in doing his work for him. She would respond only to what he said, not to what he could have said. This was her rule of thumb, and she followed it meticulously.

"Isn't it obvious?" he replied, looking Buckley in the eye and removing his glasses.

Buckley stiffened, then leaned into the microphone. "Senator, I'm sure that the delegation that presented these cases to you made an argument with them. I'd like to respond to their argument, but I need to hear it first."

"It's simple," Goethe replied, with a touch of irritation. "Keeping physician-assisted suicide illegal has not stopped people from asking for this service and sometimes getting it in one form or another." His voice began to rise. "Usually there is no physician, no proper facilities and no skills. What a horror story! We're talking about morphine being administered poorly and about suffocation. I could go further, but suffice it to say that it's a tragedy. Surely you admit that at least!"

"Yes, I do," Buckley answered, reaching for the file with her prepared response.

"Well then, Doctor," Goethe became soft and intense, speaking very slowly, "don't you think that we should get on with it and legalize this practice since it is happening anyway? That way we could bring it out into the open where we could regulate it."[1]

Legalizing and regulating suicide: more humane?

And then came the zinger, the kind of question that would put anybody on the defensive. "I ask you this," the senator said. "Wouldn't legalizing this practice make it safer for suffering people and be a mark of a civilized and compassionate society?"

As Ron sat and listened to this question, he shook his head. *He's good,* he thought to himself. *I'll give him that.* With this one very simple-sounding question the senator had positioned himself on the side of compassion and civility, leaving his opponents stuck, looking as though they opposed these commodities. Who could sit there and argue against compassion or civility? What could Buckley or Vanzanten possibly say before all these people that would avoid the appearance of doing exactly that?

Buckley was about to attempt a response when Senator Goethe grabbed the microphone and poured it on even thicker. "Is it not inhumane to ignore these botched suicides as we are doing right now?" There was another firebrand word, *inhumane.* The senator was obviously pulling out all the stops. Now he was the one on the side of humane treatment as well, leaving Buckley and Vanzanten as the ones appearing to oppose it. What could be more obvious to everyone in the room than that?

Looking up at the senator, Dr. Buckley saw that he was finished and waiting for her to respond. It would be best to ignore his comments about compassion, civility and humane treatment of people, at least for the time. She would get nowhere by touching them now and would only come off looking defensive.

There was another card to be played, the consistency card. She knew that no one was consistent all the time, but she also knew that no one wanted to be *known* or seen as inconsistent. For that reason, consistency was an important commodity to appeal to in any argument. But it was even more important than usual here because consistency was the key to evaluating this particular argument. Goethe was vulnerable on this point and Buckley knew it.

The file with her prepared response to Goethe's question lay open before her. She folded her hands together under her chin and glanced down at the file as she leaned forward on the table. "I have a question for you too," she said, looking up at Goethe.

"Yes?"

Appealing to consistency — "My question is whether or not you want to be consistent with the principle you appear to be applying in this botched-suicide argument?"

Goethe was not amused by the question. Merely asking it

implied that there was some chance that he didn't care about consistency. "Of course I want to be consistent," he growled.

Buckley grew bolder. "Then tell me if I'm wrong, but are you not assuming that the fact that someone violates a law and is harmed in the process is a good reason for changing that law to make the forbidden practice legal? That way, as you put it, 'no one would ever have to do it in secret anymore. It would be out in the open; we could regulate it, make it safer and more humane.' I believe those were your words. Didn't you just say that the reason physician-assisted suicide should be made legal is because some people are violating the law against it and being harmed in the process?" *Underlying principle of the botched-suicide argument*

Goethe shifted his weight uneasily from one side of the chair to the other. He was obviously uncomfortable with Buckley's take on his argument.

Buckley continued. "What if we were to apply your principle to other actions that are illegal? It's a simple way to test any principle to find out whether or not it should be followed. And if we apply this test to your botched-suicide argument, we will see that it falls apart." *Sixth argument opposing PAS: Botched suicides are not a reason to legalize PAS.*

Goethe frowned.

"I once read of a man," Buckley said, looking down at the file again, "who broke into a store during the night through the heating ducts. He soon found the ducts too small, and as he was sliding through he got stuck. Eventually he could move neither in nor out, and he began to suffocate. He nearly died, but the surprised business owner arrived in the morning, heard groans coming from the ceiling, and called for help."

People throughout the audience were laughing to one another. "Serves him right," the man behind Ron said to the woman with him, loudly enough for people nearby to hear him. A middle-aged woman glared back at him. Senator Ryan slammed his gavel. "Order! Order!" he barked into his microphone, and the room quieted down.

Goethe was not amused. "C'mon, Doctor!" he burst

out. "Can't you see the difference between . . ."

"Let me finish," Buckley cut in, surprising Goethe with her sudden aggressiveness. "Sure there are differences, but not relevant ones. This burglar violated a law and was harmed in the process, just as your principle states. Are you seriously suggesting that we should legalize breaking and entering so we can bring this illegal, and sometimes harmful, activity out into the open, so we can regulate it and make it more humane?"

"And are you seriously suggesting," Goethe shot back, "that breaking and entering is like physician-assisted suicide? They're not the same thing at all! How can you compare these two?"

Carefully comparing different cases: Are they similar at the points relevant for comparison? "I compare them in this way only," Buckley returned, her voice beginning to rise. "Both physician-assisted suicide and breaking and entering are illegal. Laws against both can be violated and sometimes are, and in both cases people sometimes get hurt in the process of violating them. Didn't you just pinpoint these facts about physician-assisted suicide as the reasons that it should be legalized?"

"Uh-huh."

"Then these are the relevant facts in our comparison. All the other differences don't matter. They are profoundly irrelevant because the principle you are using does not pertain to them. If you really want to get consistent with your principle, you will have to legalize breaking and entering and a host of other presently illegal actions that people sometimes perform and get hurt by in the process."

Goethe fired back, "But you're missing something, Doctor."

"And what is that?"

"You're ignoring the fact that if we legalize breaking and entering, other people will be harmed, namely, the people who are burglarized. And besides, nobody is asking to be burglarized, but those who want physician-assisted suicides are. I'll say it again: You're comparing things that are different."

Buckley shook her head. How could anyone so totally and completely miss the point like the senator just had? "No," she said flatly. "They are not different, at least not in any relevant way."

Goethe shook his head in bewilderment. "How can you just sit there and say that?"

"Because in both cases," Buckley replied, "somebody wants the liberty to do something illegal, and somebody else is being harmed by that illegal act. In a break and enter, the burglar wants to break in, and the property owner is harmed by it. In a physician-assisted suicide, someone wants to end her life with the assistance of a physician, and other people will be harmed by it."

"Who is harmed by a suffering person receiving a physician-assisted suicide?" Goethe shot back.

"The entire class of elderly, terminally ill and disabled people who would be forced to justify their own continued existence, and this at the most vulnerable time in their lives. And eventually all of us will be harmed if we travel the slippery slope as we have argued that we surely will."

"I know, I know, you've been telling us about this slippery slope and the burden we will be imposing on the elderly and the others," Goethe said with frustration, "but I don't believe any of that. I fail to see how legalizing this practice would harm anyone."

"But not believing it is not good enough," Buckley shot back, "especially for a person in your position."

"I think I understand my position, Doctor," he cut in testily.

Buckley was undeterred. "Then you know that before you implement a new public policy like this one, you have to show that our most vulnerable citizens will not be harmed by it."

Buckley paused and looked directly at Goethe. "The reason I find your botched-suicide argument unconvincing, Senator, is that where there are good reasons for any

Why the existence of botched suicides does not constitute a good reason to legalize PAS: (a) A legitimate law should not be changed simply because people are harmed as they violate it.

law, then the fact that someone violates the law and is harmed in the process is never enough reason to change that law, whether it is a law against breaking and entering, speeding, murder, rape or physician-assisted suicide. I think we all know that."

The senator muttered something to himself.

Buckley continued. "And do you know the most interesting part?"

"I can't wait to hear it."

"The flip side of that is also true. If there are no good reasons for keeping something illegal, then we don't even need something like the botched-suicide argument to set aside that law. The law shouldn't have been there in the first place."

(b) If a law is illegitimate, it should be changed even if people are not harmed by violating it.

Then Buckley grew bolder. She remembered the senator's appeal to compassion and civility at the beginning of his question, and it angered her. "There is one thing I wish to add," she said.

"Yes?"

"I do not appreciate your cavalier use of the terms *compassion, civility* and *humane treatment* as though somehow simply using these terms makes your viewpoint the compassionate or humane one."

Goethe's eyes flashed and his face reddened, but by this time Buckley didn't care. "Compassion is what our organization is all about," she continued, "and we do not use the term glibly. We would ask you and the other senators this one question about compassion."

"Uh-huh?"

"If legalizing physician-assisted suicide will impose a devastating burden on the entire class of the elderly, the terminally ill and the disabled, as we have argued, and if it will lead to other abuses, then where is the compassion in that?"

"But I've already said I don't believe any of that!"

"And I repeat that not believing something is not good enough. You must show these contentions to be unfounded. To talk glibly about compassion and civility while ignoring these very real risks to vulnerable citizens is, in our view, irresponsible."

The senator bit his tongue.

The last question came from a Senator Cooper, a small man who appeared to be in his early sixties. He had thick gray hair and wore a hearing aid that he was continually adjusting, never managing to get it quite right as the volume of the voices fluctuated greatly.

"My question is this," he began, speaking slowly in a gravelly voice, "should this practice really be called suicide?" It was pretty clear that this senator, at least, did not think so, and his next words erased any doubt. "Do you not think that this is an unnecessarily negative term used to distort this practice in the minds of people, and to turn them against it without even so much as an argument?" *Is the use of the word* suicide *a semantic ploy to turn people against PAS?*

This point had been made rather effectively by the delegation from Academics for Social Justice on Monday, and Vanzanten remembered it well. They had argued that the word *suicide* is not the appropriate term because most suicides are so different from what happens when a physician helps a suffering person end his life of suffering. Vanzanten and Buckley were glad for the opportunity to respond to the argument. *Is PAS really suicide?*

"In our view," Vanzanten replied, "things should be called what they are. Doing anything else is playing the semantics game, which distorts issues and misleads people." *We should call things what they are.*

"Good," said the senator. "Then perhaps you'll agree with me that the word *suicide* should not be used to describe the practice we are debating."

"Actually," replied Vanzanten, "I'm having trouble seeing what is wrong with the term."

Cooper held his microphone with both hands. "Can you not see the difference between most acts of suicide and what happens when a physician aids a suffering person in ending his life peacefully?"

Vanzanten took a quick breath. "Perhaps you could tell

us *exactly* how physician-assisted suicide is different from other cases of suicide?" he asked.

Differences between PAS and most other suicides

"In a suicide," replied Cooper, "usually a long life is cut short by the impulsive act of a person temporarily overcome with depression, leaving loved ones overcome with grief and guilt. Furthermore, if the attempt is unsuccessful, the person is usually glad she was rescued and wants to live. Suicide ends a *living* process. What we are talking about here ends the *dying* process of a person whose death is already under way. The person has thought it through and prepared for it. Furthermore, she would want to go on living if it were not for the illness or condition that has driven her to this point."

"That is true for all suicide victims, Senator," Vanzanten cut in. "They would all want to go on living if it were not for the condition or circumstances that had driven them to this point."[2]

"All right, I'll give you that," Cooper replied, "but can you not see the difference between this practice and what we normally call suicide?"

"Yes, there are differences, important ones. I'll readily acknowledge that."

"Well then?" Cooper raised his hands.

"What interests me is whether or not there are any differences that make physician-assisted suicide no longer suicide. Remember, that is all we're talking about. The definition of *suicide*."

"What's that now?" Cooper leaned forward intently and cocked his head sideways.

But PAS still involves essential characteristics of suicide.

"Do any of the differences you have set out," repeated Vanzanten, "affect the definition of the word *suicide*? That is the only relevant question here since we're asking whether the term *suicide* should be used to describe this practice."

Cooper shrugged and nodded.

"Correct me if I'm wrong, Senator, but I see nothing in any of the differences you have given us that change this practice from being a suicide. It is still the act of a person, for his own reasons, ending his own life and doing so with the help of a physician. That is suicide. Sure, there are differences, but that only means there are different kinds of suicides."

Vanzanten paused and leaned over to Buckley, who was whispering something in his ear. He nodded and returned to his microphone. "With all due respect, Senator, we see this attempt to drop the term *suicide* as producing exactly the kind of result you spoke of earlier. It is an attempt by advocates of physician-assisted suicide to hide from people the reality of what is happening and to slant them in favor of the practice without even an argument."

Is avoiding the word suicide a semantic ploy to turn people in favor of PAS?

Vanzanten had barely finished speaking when Ryan hurriedly moved to cut off the debate. He grabbed his microphone and announced a ten-minute recess before hearing the last delegation, Not Dead Yet. The sound of his gavel ricocheted off the walls and sent people rushing to the outer hallway in search of phones, rest rooms, fresh air and a chance to stretch their muscles.

As Ron stood he noticed a well-dressed man in a wheelchair being pushed through the crowd toward the delegates' table by another man, who was speaking to him as they went. A third person, an older woman, was walking ahead of them, carrying a document case and talking on a cellular phone. Eventually the little entourage arrived at the table, where the woman continued to talk on the phone while the other two arranged the wheelchair in place and set the open document case on the table.

The three of them conversed together quietly as TV cameras began to focus in on them. One reporter who ventured too close was authoritatively waved back by the man who had pushed the wheelchair.

As Ron watched the man in the wheelchair, he thought of Patrick, who was heading down the same road in life. He would also be in a wheelchair soon, that is if he chose to live, and yet here was this man about to tell the world why he opposed the legalization of physician-assisted suicide. Ron shook his head and walked outside for a breath of fresh air.

17

The sound of Ryan's gavel rapping repeatedly interrupted the commotion in the hearings room. "Order! Order!" he was calling out. He leaned forward close to his microphone, squinting at the crowd of people. "We have one final delegation," he said. "Not Dead Yet. This group is represented here today by Mr. Malcolm Macintosh. Please go ahead, sir, and begin by telling us something about your group."

The man in the wheelchair leaned forward. He appeared to be in his early forties and had a full head of carefully styled hair. His well-pressed navy sports jacket and tie gave him a professional look.

"Thank you, sir," he said crisply. "We are an organization of disabled people, and our purpose is to communicate a message to our fellow citizens."

This interested Ryan. "And what message is that?"

"It is that we, the disabled, are real people," he said slowly, "with real and, yes, rewarding lives." He paused and looked directly at Ryan. "*Disabled* does not mean *dead,* nor does being disabled bring an end to a life worth living." Ryan's eyes darted back and forth at his colleagues, gauging their reaction. Most were nodding and glancing at one another, giving this disabled man a sympathetic ear.

Disabled life can be rewarding.

"Oh sure," Macintosh said, "we have struggles that able-bodied people do not have. I guess that's obvious, isn't it?" He motioned toward his wheelchair with both hands. "But the fact is that we *all* have struggles, whatever

Even able bodied people are not exempt from life's struggles.

our physical condition happens to be. *We* have to deal with ours and *you* all have to deal with yours."

Ryan's chin was resting in both hands, and his eyes were glued to Macintosh. "That is certainly food for thought," he replied.

Macintosh looked down at the file before him, then suddenly closed it, looking up again. "I have a prepared statement," he said, "but I would rather speak without notes today."

"From the heart," Ryan smiled.

"You might say so." Macintosh leaned forward, hands tightly folded on the table, and looked back and forth across the row of legislators elevated before him. "Senators," he said, "you have a heavy responsibility placed upon you by the voters. Most of us do not envy you. In a few short days, you will cast your votes, and these votes will have the power to change the world for thousands of people. You will decide whether or not physician-assisted suicide will become a legal and available option for suffering people in our society." He paused and shook his head, as if the significance of these legislators' responsibility was just now sinking in.

Ryan smiled and nodded, almost appreciatively, as if he was thankful that finally, here was someone who understood the weight of the decisions he and his colleagues had to make year after year. "Thank you for noticing."

Macintosh nodded in return. "There are times," he continued, "when I wish you could make this decision, could cast your vote, from the perspective of a person in this chair." He motioned again to his wheelchair.

Ron glanced around at the people near him. All were mesmerized by this man in the wheelchair. You could have heard a pin drop in the huge hearings room.

"Four years ago," Macintosh proceeded, "I was where all of you are today, the picture of health. I played squash three times each week and loved it. It was something I looked forward to. I hiked and rode a mountain bike on the weekends, and I was planning to take up water skiing.

The ski boat was already sitting in my garage. My family and I loved the outdoors.

"Then one day I noticed that something was not right. A feeling of numbness had come across my face and would not go away. It persisted, and soon I began losing proper coordination and strength. I began dropping dishes for no reason. My brisk walk turned to a shuffle, and I no longer trusted myself on a bicycle. A battery of tests showed that I have multiple sclerosis, a disease that brings gradual deterioration in the use of muscles and in other bodily functions. It was a disease I dreaded." *The grief and losses experienced by the disabled*

Ryan was writing furiously on his legal pad and whispering occasional comments to the aide sitting directly behind him, who was also scrawling notes on a legal pad.

Macintosh took a drink from the glass on the table, carefully swished the water around in his mouth, then took another sip, and just as carefully, set the glass down again. "Soon I lost my voice," he continued, "then I regained it. Then I lost it again and, as you can see, I have regained it once more." Then he laughed. "There are people today who wish I would lose it again, once and for all."

A smattering of nervous laughter was heard throughout the audience. The man had obviously not lost his sense of humor, or if he had, it too had returned. He continued on, spelling out in graphic detail his journey from able-bodied life to life in this wheelchair. He spoke of the pain and the loss of abilities and opportunities he had hoped to pursue. This was not what he had expected out of life. It was not what life was supposed to have been like.

As Ron looked around again and studied the looks on people's faces, he could see immense respect being generated for this man who had endured so much. These able-bodied people could only wonder how they would respond if it were them sitting in that wheelchair. The more Macintosh told of his own story, the greater the respect and almost admiration that seemed to be coming from these people.

Ron looked toward the front again. "Eventually I was

introduced to one of these," Macintosh was saying, pointing a third time to his wheelchair.

Ryan had not stopped writing. He looked up briefly, then down again, and wrote some more.

"Most of the activities that previously gave me pleasure and enjoyment," he said, "I could no longer do. I began to feel trapped in a body that didn't work. It was like *I* was here and my *body* was over there." He gestured first to himself, then to the seat beside him.

"My grief was unimaginable, and I began to wonder why I should carry on. What was the point? When I tried to encourage myself, all I could think of was that things would only get worse as time went on. Each passing month would bring the loss of more bodily functions and abilities. I was on a downhill track and there was nothing I could do to stop the train."

Many faces in the audience were ashen. Never before had they so carefully contemplated the process of going from able-bodied health to a disabled condition. Macintosh was holding nothing back as he told his story.

Ryan was also moved by the story. His glasses were in his hand, and he rubbed his eyes. "Mr. Macintosh," he said sincerely, "you speak eloquently. I for one am learning much from your presentation. Could you explain to us, precisely, how this very powerful story has influenced your views on physician-assisted suicide?"

Macintosh nodded and took another sip of water from the glass. "Let me put it this way, Senator. This grief went on for over a year."

"That's a long time," Ryan said, immediately realizing the emptiness of such a statement and wishing he had not made it.

The danger in offering PAS to a person experiencing grief and loss

"And I am here to say to all of you today that I am profoundly grateful that no one came to me during that time and offered me 'death with dignity.' Because I would almost certainly have taken it. My judgment could not be trusted during that time, just as most other suicidal people's judgment cannot be trusted at the moment they want to die. I was too heartbroken. The emotional trauma was simply too great."

Ryan leaned forward. "For the record then, you are here in opposition to legalizing physician-assisted suicide? Is that correct?"

"Yes. I hope and pray that you will not legalize this practice."

Ryan nodded, breathed deeply and tilted his head. "But if I may say so with the greatest of respect, Mr. Macintosh, you have pinpointed the exact reasons why some of us have come to believe that this practice *should* be legalized."

Macintosh sat upright. "How did I do that, Senator?"

Ryan picked up his notes, adjusted his glasses and flipped back a few pages. "You just told us that as a result of your disability, you could no longer do most of the activities that previously gave you enjoyment."

But isn't the plight of the disabled reason enough to give them the choice to die?

"Yes, that's right."

"You felt trapped in your body, I believe those were your words. It seemed as if you were here, and your body was over there. As you put it, your grief was unimaginable, and all you had to look forward to was even further deterioration. Is this a fair rendition of what you said?"

"You take careful notes, Senator."

"In this job you have to," he joked. Then turning serious again, he said, "Your story has been very descriptive, but frankly, Mr. Macintosh, as I said, it is descriptions just like yours that have led some of us to believe we ought to make the option of choosing physician-assisted suicide available for people who are facing the kind of suffering and hopelessness you have so forcefully described."

Macintosh listened closely, tapping his pencil on the table but saying nothing.

"I think I speak for all of my colleagues," Ryan continued, "when I say that we have no idea what it must be like to experience the kind of grief and loss that you have experienced. My hat is off to you, sir. I have the deepest compassion for anyone who finds himself in this kind of circumstance."

"Thank you, Senator." Macintosh seemed genuinely moved.

"But that is precisely why I, for one, believe we should, out of compassion, offer people who face this kind of hopeless suffering at least the choice of ending their suffering gently and peacefully if they wish to. Does not compassion require that we offer them the same choice that most of us would want if we were facing these painful circumstances?"

Ryan stopped speaking and the room was deathly quiet. Malcolm Macintosh had stopped tapping his pencil. He put it down, folded his hands before him and looked up at Ryan. "In that case, Senator," he said softly, "may I ask you where your compassion is for the able-bodied thirty- or forty-year-old man who finds himself in his own deeply distressing circumstances and wants to end *his* suffering through suicide?"

Ryan looked confused, unclear of why Macintosh was asking questions about able-bodied people.

Calling for consistency: Shouldn't the *able-bodied* who also suffer be given the same choice?

"Perhaps it's a family breakup," Macintosh continued, "or the loss of a parent or a child or a special relationship. Maybe it stems from early abuse, or financial devastation, or from being a loner. My question to you is, where is your compassion for *this* kind of suffering person?" He looked into Ryan's eyes, and waited for him to answer.

Ryan was at a loss as to how to respond. "I have the deepest sympathy for these unfortunate ones too," he finally said.

Macintosh pressed further. "But do you believe we should give them the option of ending their suffering through suicide? Better yet," he said, his voice rising, "do you believe we should actually *help* these suicidal people end their lives?"

"Of course not!" Ryan answered emphatically, still not knowing why Macintosh was taking him down this path. "They need our *help*, when they find themselves down on their luck, to get through a difficult time. They need hope.

They need the best suicide prevention measures we can bring them. Surely, you're not saying that . . ."

"What I'm saying, Senator, is that when you were speaking of *disabled* people who are suffering, you told us that compassion requires you to give them—or should I say, give *us*—the option of ending our suffering through suicide assistance. If you were one of us, you said, you would want that option for yourself, so you felt it should be offered to others who are disabled."

"Uh-huh."

"But now you are telling us you would not provide the same suicide assistance for suffering *able-bodied* people who also want to die."

Ryan nodded.

"And I'm asking where your compassion is for these *able-bodied* people who also want to die because of their own painful circumstances. They, too, see their lives as hopeless, not worth living, and want to end them. Please tell me, Senator, if compassion requires you to offer suicide assistance in one case, then why not in the other?" *Why would we offer PAS to the disabled but not to the able-bodied?*

Ryan sighed and looked down, squinting and rubbing his eyes again. Then he leaned back and whispered something to the aide behind him, who whispered something back. He had nothing to say just yet, he said, and motioned for Macintosh to continue.

"With all due respect, sir," Macintosh said, "are you forgetting that if you were in the place of the forty-year-old suicidal person I spoke of, you would equally want that choice to die? These people, and they do exist, really want to die, and if you or I were them, we would too."

Ryan cleared his throat, unsure of what to say at this point. He whispered again to the aide, who began thumbing through a thick file filled with documents.

Macintosh leaned forward and pushed farther. "By your own account, Senator, you are giving different treatment to the *able-bodied* than to the *disabled.*" He paused and studied the row of senators. Some were writing furiously. A few were nodding with enthusiastic agreement. It was obvious that to quite a few of them, these were new concepts altogether. Ryan slumped back in his chair, no longer writing.

Then Macintosh's voice rose. "Don't you see, Senator, that you just made a value judgment about the worth of a disabled human life? It looks very much like you have judged it to be less worth fighting for than an able-bodied life. I say that because you just said that when an able-bodied person sees life as hopeless and wants to die, he should receive suicide *prevention*. His request to die should be denied, you said, and we should fight for his life with the best suicide-prevention measures we have. But when a *disabled* person sees life in the same way and becomes suicidal, you said this person should receive suicide *assistance*. Do you see the difference, Senator?"

Seventh argument opposing PAS: Legalizing PAS results in the devaluing of disabled and ill people.

Ryan frowned and rubbed his chin, looking back and forth at his colleagues. Suddenly the aide behind him leaned forward and whispered something in his ear. Ryan raised his hand to Macintosh, motioning him to stop. Then he hurriedly swiveled his chair around and formed a quick huddle with the aide and the senator on either side of him.

The other two senators were animated; they were speaking at the same time, shaking their heads vehemently and jabbing the air to punctuate their words. Ryan was listening and nodding. Soon he returned to his microphone with a somber expression on his face.

"Mr. Macintosh," he said slowly, his voice rich with intensity. "I must tell you in the most emphatic terms that neither I nor any of my colleagues on this committee believe that disabled human life has less value than able-bodied life, as you seem to suggest." As he spoke, he waved both arms at the long row of senators, then squinted down at Macintosh.

A number of the senators across the front were nodding aggressively. They had obviously grasped this disabled man's point and understood it all too well. A few were clearly offended by it.

Macintosh was unfazed and unrepentant. "With all due respect to you, sir, and to your colleagues, I believe you."

Ryan looked surprised. "You what?"

"I believe you," Macintosh repeated. "I never said that you were consciously intending to make a distinction in value between disabled life and able-bodied life."

Ryan threw up his hands, looking back and forth at his colleagues again. "What then?"

"I'm sure you consciously hold to the equality of all human life."

"Yes, I do!" Ryan practically shouted.

"And you would explicitly deny that disabled life has less value."

"Yes, I would deny that!"

"But your different responses to the disabled and the able-bodied are telling a different story. They are making a statement."

Ryan pulled off his glasses. "What story? What statement?"

"Both the able-bodied person and the disabled person I just mentioned were suffering. Both saw life as hopeless and both were suicidal. You decided that the *able-bodied* life was worth fighting for even if it meant denying the suffering person his request to die. But you decided none of that for the *disabled* person. Somehow, compassion required you to grant suicide assistance for her. It's hard to avoid the conclusion that disabled human life is being valued less, or at least is considered less worth fighting for, than able-bodied life, regardless of your statements to the contrary."[1]

Our *actions*, not our *words*, tell the real story about how we value able-bodied and disabled life.

Macintosh cleared his throat and looked down, speaking almost into the table. "As you can well imagine, Senators, some of us in the disabled community feel this directly. We know full well how most people feel about the quality of our lives in the first place. How often we have heard people say that if they were in our wheelchairs, they would want the choice to end it all, when they would never say any such thing about an able-bodied person who is also suffering and wanting to die."

Then he paused, looking earnestly into the faces of a few individual senators. "What we are really here to ask you, Senators," he said, "is that you value disabled life in the same way that you value able-bodied life, that you treat our lives as just as worth fighting for, and just as worth living, as if we were able-bodied."

Then he looked up again, focusing on the row of senators. "Perhaps you can see now why our organization exists. Disability does not equal death. We are disabled. We are not dead. Nor do our disabilities spell the end of a life worth living."

Suddenly Macintosh's eyes flashed and he pulled out a small stack of academic journals and began waving them at the row of senators. "It's all here!" he exclaimed. "If you don't believe me, read these!"

Ryan squinted across the distance to Macintosh, trying to see what the small books were. "And what are those?"

"These contain the story of how most disabled people rate their own quality of life." Macintosh was still waving the journals.

This intrigued Ryan. "And how is that?" he asked.

"Disabled people rate their own quality of life virtually identically to the way able-bodied people rate theirs. The same!" he said emphatically, leaning close to the microphone.[2]

Ryan looked surprised. "I must admit, I never would have expected that," he mumbled.

"And the same research," Macintosh carried on, again raising the journals, "tells another story as well."

Ryan shrugged and shook his head. "What story?"

"The story of how able-bodied people rate the quality of life of disabled people."

Ryan sat upright, fearing the worst. "How?"

"Very low." He punched out the words, one at a time. Then leaning back, he asked, "Do you see why the word 'compassion' actually scares some of us in this community? Do you see why we're not so sure we *want* the compassion of people who think our lives are hardly worth living, who repeatedly say that if they had our lives, they would want the option of ending them, when these same people would never say any such thing about able-bodied people who also suffer and want to die?"

Ryan flinched. He had done precisely what Macintosh was describing, and had used the word *compassion* to boot. These words were directed at him, and he knew it.

Macintosh was finished speaking and was leaning back, sipping on his glass of water again. Ryan decided this conversation had gone on long enough. In fact, the hearings had gone on long enough for him, and it was time to bring them to an end. As he was shuffling through his notes in search of his closing comments, he noticed another senator on his far left signaling him, wanting to ask Macintosh a follow-up question.

Senator Ryan frowned. Further discussion was the very thing he secretly wanted to avoid. He knew how volatile things could get with the disabled man sitting there, publicly implying that Ryan and some of his colleagues were devaluing disabled human life. Could he afford to open the floor and hope for the best? But on the other hand, could he afford not to? He knew he would run the risk of looking like he wanted to cut off discussion of this issue. He looked quickly at the other senator, then down again, then reluctantly gave her the floor.

18

Her name was Senator Ellen Goy, a highly professional-looking woman in her early fifties who gave every appearance of having been a lecturer or negotiator earlier in her life. She wore oval-shaped wire-rimmed glasses and had a short, contemporary hairstyle, revealing eye-catching silver earrings that sparkled in the lights of the hearing room. Known for her pro-business views, she was a force to be reckoned with in senate debates and was someone the business community could count on.

She was on record as being undecided on this particular issue and no one in the room could predict what kind of question she might ask a person like Macintosh. Holding her glasses in her hands, she leaned forward into her microphone. After pausing for a few seconds that seemed more like a few minutes, she spit out the words, "But what about animals?"

At first Macintosh was baffled. He shrugged, raised both hands in the air and looked at the people around him. "Could you help me out here a little, Senator?"

"Mr. Macintosh," she said, curtly yet respectfully, "you have painted a graphic picture of the suffering that disabled people endure."

Macintosh nodded.

"You have given most of us here today a new appreciation for the obstacles that life throws in the path of thousands of disabled people like yourself."

Senators across the front nodded thoughtfully in agreement.

She slipped her glasses on, looked down at her legal pad and flipped through a couple of pages. Still looking down, she said, half reading, "But of course, suffering, pain and the obstacles of life are not limited to the disabled. You've also shown us that today."

Macintosh took another drink of water and wiped his mouth. He had no clue where this senator was going with her comments. She was obviously highly experienced in the art of debate and dialogue. "Yes, that's correct," he replied, trying to relax.

The senator again pulled off her glasses and looked down at Macintosh. "Many people are tragically afflicted with painful and sometimes terminal diseases. There are brain tumors, aneurysms and spinal cord fractures. There is leukemia, AIDS and cancer," she said, with greater than average sincerity. Her next words told why.

"Unfortunately," she said, "I happen to have very recent first-hand experience with the suffering that these diseases can bring on a person, especially in their final stages. I have just returned from my own father's funeral. He lost his battle with throat cancer."

Macintosh was suddenly much more interested in what this senator had to say on the topic of human suffering. "I'm sorry," he said, barely above a whisper.

"And I have to tell you, Mr. Macintosh, that especially after this experience, something bothers me deeply about the way we treat suffering people."

Macintosh leaned forward and listened intently. "What is that?" he queried.

"It appears to me," she said slowly, stressing each word, "and please correct me if I'm wrong, but it looks very much like we treat them worse than we treat our animals who are suffering."

Ron perked up his ears. This was exactly what Patrick had told him on the day Ron had arrived at his home. It had bothered him ever since. He thought of Patrick's black Labradors that had been resting on the floor providing the perfect object lesson for Patrick's argument.

In refusing to grant PAS to them, do we treat suffering people worse than suffering animals?

No matter how hard he had tried to discount or ignore this point, Ron could see no way of denying that this is exactly what we do in our society. We *should* treat animals well. Ron believed that. But *better* than humans? How could that be right? If animals deserved to be treated with compassion in their suffering, didn't humans deserve at least that much?"

Macintosh, too, had suddenly caught on to where the senator was heading and began reaching for a file that he hoped would offer him some help. He looked up at the senator. "Treating humans worse than animals," he said. "I don't like the sound of that. How are we doing it?"

Treating animals humanely: ending their suffering

The senator slipped her glasses on once more and quickly turned another page in her legal pad. "Again, correct me if I'm wrong," she said, "but when animals in our society suffer greatly, we put them out of their misery . . . quickly." Her voice rose slightly. "We do not let them linger on and on." Then she spoke louder, with great emphasis. "But do you know what really gets to me, what really makes my blood boil about this, Mr. Macintosh?"

He didn't, of course.

"It's the *reason* we do not allow animals to linger on in their suffering."

"The reason?"

"Yes, Mr. Macintosh. Do you know what the reason is?"

Again, he did not. He was tempted to try some answer about our duty to be kind to animals, but decided it would probably fall flat with this hard-hitting senator. He shook his head.

"It is because we have decided we ought to treat animals *humanely.*" Her voice rose substantially higher on that word. She said it again. *"Humanely!"*

Ron's head was slowly shaking. This senator knew how to make a point—and then make it again even more powerfully. At that moment, he was very glad to be sitting where he was and not at the table like Macintosh.

Goy probed further. "Does it not strike you as odd that we stop the suffering of *animals* because we want to treat them humanely, but we allow *human* beings—our own friends and neighbors—who are suffering to linger on and on, even when they go so far as to ask us to help them end it through a gentle and peaceful death? Does this not seem odd or backward to you, Mr. Macintosh?"

By now Goy was passionate, and Macintosh was feeling very warm.

"Is it just me," she continued, "or is something seriously out of sync here?" She put down the legal pad she had been holding and leaned back in her chair, waiting for Macintosh to say something, anything.

This was not exactly a new argument to Macintosh. He had encountered it before, but he had never heard it expressed as eloquently or dramatically as this, and he certainly had never had to respond to it in front of a few hundred people including reporters and TV camera crews.

A file folder now lay open before him, and he began paging through it slowly, struggling for the best way to reply. He could feel the stares from the room full of people as his body temperature continued to rise. He now knew why this was called the hot seat. *I wonder how many of them feel sorry for me,* he thought. *Are they wondering if I'll be able to respond to the challenge? Will I be able to?*

Seconds passed, and finally Ryan looked at him questioningly. "Mr. Macintosh, would you care to respond to the senator?"

Macintosh nodded and eventually leaned forward to the microphone. He tried to sound convincing.

"This bothered me too, Senator, . . . at first."

"At first?" Goy sounded doubtful.

Macintosh nodded. "Yes. Our willingness to help a suffering animal die but not a suffering human bothered me."

"OK," she said slowly, in a questioning tone. "I take it you've gotten over it?"

"Let's just say that my thinking changed a couple of years ago when somebody passed on to me an old proverb." This seemed like a good place to start even though he couldn't be sure where it would take him.

Eighth
argument
opposing PAS:
Differences
between
animals and
humans make
the
comparison
between them
illegitimate.

Goy also wondered where this conversation was going. "And the proverb is . . ."

"Never tear down an old fence post until you find out why it was put there in the first place."

The senator nodded slowly, unsure of what this proverb meant or why anyone would mention it here. "Perhaps you'll tell us what your proverb means?"

"Oh, it's not *my* proverb," he laughed nervously, "but here is what it meant, to me at least, when I heard it. Our laws have always allowed us to put down suffering animals as an act of mercy."

"Yes."

"But we have always had laws prohibiting us from assisting another human being who wants to die in ending his life."

"My point exactly!"

"So, I began to inquire *why* we have, and always *have* had, this law in place prohibiting us from doing that. In fact, as you know, Senator, helping another person die has always been viewed as so wrong that the penalty for it is a prison term. Why is that? Why not just strike down that law and make it legal to help another person die? After all, as you say, we do it for animals. Why not for humans as well?"

This made Goy smile. "Mr. Macintosh, I couldn't have said it better myself."

Macintosh returned the smile. "Then it struck me," he continued, "that before we tear down this law, we should probably find out why it was put there in the first place."

Goy raised both hands in a questioning gesture and shook her head. "Well then, what did you find out? Why was it put there?"

Macintosh again glanced at his file and flipped a couple of pages, chuckling quietly to himself. *How ironic,* he thought. *A lawmaker asking me to explain why certain laws are on the books.* Luckily, he was prepared with a couple of reasons he had heard. There had to be more, but he was no lawyer, and this was the best he could do.

"Imagine," he said, "homicide detectives being called

to a home where they find a dead person—and another person who quickly says to them, 'He asked me to do it.'"

A slight murmur went over the crowd.

"How," Macintosh asked, "are those detectives ever going to begin that investigation?"

Goy was quick to respond. "But that is hardly like physician-assisted suicide for a suffering person."

"Oh yes," agreed Macintosh, "there are differences, but this does get at the reason we have laws prohibiting one person from helping another person die, when we do not have the same prohibitions against putting animals down. That *was* your argument wasn't it?" he asked, flipping back a few pages in his own notes, "That because it is legal to end the lives of suffering animals, it should be legal to do the same for suffering people?" He waited for Goy to answer.

Reasons for prohibiting humans from helping each other die that do not apply to animals

She paused and finally said, "Yes, that's what I said."

Macintosh nodded. He knew full well that this was her argument and he wasn't ready to have her disown it now.

He continued, "We prohibit people from helping other people die in order to protect us all from actually being *murdered* by someone who then uses this 'he asked me to do it' defense. After all, the only person who could possibly deny that he asked him to do it is now dead and unavailable for further comment."

(a) To prevent murderers from using a "he asked me to do it" defense

This amused Goy, and she managed a brief laugh as she quickly considered the implications of giving lawyers a 'he asked me to do it' defense for clients accused of murder. If such a defense were available, lawyers would try to use it wherever possible. She knew that. What is more, they would use it not because they were bad, sleazy lawyers, but precisely because they were good lawyers. It was their job to use every legal means at their disposal to defend their clients. Anything less would be unethical at the very least and could even get them disbarred. She made a quick note on her legal pad to consider this further at a later time.

"But there's another reason for this law," Macintosh was saying.

"Yes?"

(b) To prevent
suicidal people
from making
the worst
decision of
their lives
"It's there also to protect a suicidal person from being 'helped,'" Macintosh raised two fingers on each hand to put this word in quotation marks, "by a friend in making the worst decision of her life at a time of serious depression and suffering. Suicidal people need our help to get them *through* these very difficult periods in their lives. They need protection from people who just might be willing to 'help' them make this grave mistake."

Macintosh took a long drink of water and cleared his throat. "If I may say so, Senator," he said, "these seem like good reasons, to me, for telling our citizens they may not help another person die even though they may do so for animals. The people who wrote this law knew what they were doing, don't you think?"

Goy was looking down and scribbling notes. "Yes, I suppose so," she said without looking up.

"My point," Macintosh continued, "is that human beings are different from animals."

"Of course they are, Mr. Macintosh." She was visibly irritated that he thought he needed to tell her this, as if she might not know it already.

Animals and
humans: not a
correct
comparison
"Which means," said Macintosh, "that to compare animals and humans and simply argue that because we help animals die, therefore we should also help humans die, is a mistake. It is not a fair comparison because there are reasons for not allowing us to help other *people* die that do not apply to *animals.* In other words, the fact that we put animals down does not necessarily mean that we ought to do the same for humans."

"The bottom line," Macintosh replied, eager to wrap this up, "is that we need more reasons for helping suffering humans die than simply the fact that we help animals die, as you have argued."

"Yes," Goy responded. "You keep saying that."

"I keep saying it because we think that it is a very serious matter to remove these laws and begin to allow one group of people, physicians, to do exactly that. If we do, we will be tearing down much more than a fence post. We will be destroying the pillars of protection for those of us who have illnesses and disabilities. We implore you to leave these pillars in place."

Macintosh leaned back in his chair. He was finished speaking and was becoming tired. Goy's time was up, so Ryan leaned forward and thanked the senator and Macintosh for an exchange that he had obviously found very enlightening. "That's great stuff!" he exclaimed. Then he shook his head in relief. They had made it through Goy's time without an outburst or a flare up. This was good.

He reached for the gavel. Finally the hearings were about to come to an end, and he was smiling. Just then another senator, a short, bald, nondescript man on Ryan's far right began waving his arms wildly, calling for an opportunity to ask this disabled man one last question.

This can't be happening, Senator Ryan thought, but his colleague was impossible to ignore. He was leaning as far forward over the table as his short, stocky frame would allow, looking at Ryan and still waving.

Ron could just make out the senator's name plate from where he sat in the audience. "Sen. R. T. Cousins," it read. *He's aggressive if he's anything,* Ron thought.

Cousins looked over at Ryan, who was shaking his head firmly. There would be no more speakers or questions. He wanted to adjourn the hearings, once and for all. But the stocky senator would have none of it. "Question! Question!" he was yelling loudly enough for everyone in the room to hear him even though his microphone was not turned on.

A loud buzz erupted throughout the room as people began voicing their displeasure with a moderator who would disallow debate and discussion on such an issue. Three elderly men in the back actually rose to their feet and pointed at Ryan, yelling something totally indecipherable. They shook their heads in disbelief. Ryan sighed deeply, glanced at his watch again, then looked over at this colleague and held up five fingers. "Five minutes!" he said with finality. He pounded the table with the gavel and brought the room to order.

19

Senator Cousins was smiling enthusiastically as he took the floor.

"Mr. Macintosh!" he barked, as if he had forgotten that he no longer needed to fight for the floor. "Can we just sit here and ignore the wishes of our citizens?"

Macintosh was confused. "I hope not," he finally answered nervously, with a smirk, hoping he wasn't blindly stepping into a carefully laid trap. It had suddenly become clear to him that the citizens were in no mood to be ignored.

"Well, it appears to me that we've been studiously avoiding reality in these hearings."

This confused Macintosh even more. "I have no idea what you are talking about," he blurted out, raising his hands in the air, "and I certainly have no intention of avoiding reality, sir!"

"That may be your stated intention, sir," Cousins shot back, "but I have attended these hearings from the beginning and listened carefully to all the arguments on both sides of this issue. I have taken copious notes," he added, waving three legal pads at Macintosh, "and I can tell you that only one group in these entire hearings has even raised the question of what the people of this country might want concerning physician-assisted suicide."

Macintosh could neither verify nor deny this statement, so he let it pass.

"That group favored legalizing this practice," Cousins added, pausing dramatically for a few seconds. "I have to tell you, sir," he went on, "that I have yet to hear the opponents of legalization mention the people's wishes even once."

A soft murmur moved through the audience, and Macintosh knew Cousins had scored one, fair and square. This issue should not have been neglected by the opponents of euthanasia.

"I, for one, am unwilling to cast my vote either way," Cousins continued, "without carefully considering what the people of my constituency and of this country want on this issue. After all, it's not *my* country, it's *theirs,* and they will have to live with whatever decision we make. So maybe we should be willing to live with whatever decision they have already made. And they *have* made their decision, believe me!"

Should popular opinion dictate public policy on PAS?

Macintosh had been writing as fast as he could but looked up at the senator just then. "And what decision have they made?" he queried.

Cousins looked dumbfounded. "Have you not seen the polls on this issue?"

"Yes, as a matter of fact, I have."

"Then I hardly need to tell you what they say." He looked down and began flipping through yet another legal pad, quickly locating the page he wanted. "But I will."

People throughout the room were looking at one another and laughing, pointing up at Cousins. They were enjoying him. He was unconventional. He spoke from the heart and was brash; he was breathing new life into these hearings even in their final moments. Senator Ryan's eyes darted nervously across the room.

Then, in short, clipped sentences, Cousins began announcing the results of a number of polls and surveys taken on people's opinions on legalizing physician-assisted suicide. "Gallup, 1994." His voice rang out, "A majority in favor. Harris, 1996. Again, a majority. CNN/*Time,* 1997, a majority. In Canada, *Macleans* and Decima, 1998, a majority!"

Cousins had intended this to be startling and dramatic,

an effective way to end the hearings. But he did not expect audience participation. As he was announcing the poll results, pent-up emotions throughout the room began to spill over as people were unable to contain their enthusiasm.

"Yes!" one man shouted when Cousins was finished reading the list. Some people actually clapped and laughed with the people near them. Still others looked directly at Macintosh, shaking their heads in sympathy and amazement.

Ryan slammed down his gavel. "Order! Order!" he said sternly. Then his attitude softened and he spoke more quietly, "Ladies and gentlemen, we have all been here a long time. You have been very patient and respectful, and I thank you. These hearings are almost over, and it is of utmost importance that we complete them with the same order that we have maintained throughout. In a very few minutes you will have an opportunity to speak your minds, and, as I said earlier, members of the media, who are already at the door, will be more than happy to hear you then." He chuckled as people sat back and smiled.

Smooth, Ron thought. *No wonder he's made it to this lofty office.*

Ryan thanked the audience once more for their courtesy and turned the floor back to Cousins, who was not about to exhibit the same kind of generosity.

"Mr. Moderator," he barked. "My time has been cut into and I ask you for a three-minute extension."

Ryan shook his head in frustrated amazement and let out a deep sigh, shaking his head. "Could the timekeeper please add three minutes to the senator's time?" he droned into his microphone.

"Thank you, Mr. Moderator," Cousins returned, seemingly oblivious to Ryan's displeasure. Then he turned back toward Macintosh, who was digging through his briefcase, searching for another file.

Cousins, charged by the obvious support he was receiving, could barely contain himself. "Is it as clear to you as it is to me, Mr. Macintosh?" he asked loudly, both hands raised in the air. "Regardless of the reasons you or any other delegation have brought, it is clear that the people want this service to be available. They want it legalized!" Now he dragged out each word. "Now the last time I checked, we live in a democracy, where the people have the final say."

This comment irritated Macintosh. Of course it was a democracy. He knew that and didn't need any tongue-in-cheek lecture about things that anyone with a pulse should know.

Cousins carried on. "Mr. Macintosh, you have a right to your views on this topic or any other. What you do not have a right to do is to force your views about what is acceptable or unacceptable on the majority of citizens who disagree with you. That is what democracy is all about, sir!" With that, he sat back and waited for Macintosh to respond. *Should a minority view ever become law?*

Cousins was glad he had been able to make this point and drive it home with the help of his polls. Even better, he was able to do it as the last argument, leaving the audience and the country thinking about this democratic principle as the hearings adjourned. Things could not have worked out better. At the end of the day, he reasoned, what could be more powerful than this argument from the nature of democracy? This was the real trump card and he was more than happy to have played it now.

He looked at Macintosh, who was quietly looking down at the file he had finally located in the attaché case and flipping very slowly through its contents. But what could Macintosh say to this argument? What could anyone? After all, shouldn't the people themselves be able to decide their own fate in matters of morality and social policy?

Who would dare come before hearings like these and argue that the views of a minority should be foisted on the majority, especially on a moral issue like this? Surely anyone who tried it would attract profound disdain and would have his credibility ruined.

The room was deathly quiet as Cousins and advocates

of assisted suicide throughout the audience eased forward in their chairs, anticipating Macintosh's imminent and very public defeat. They hoped it would mean the defeat of his viewpoint as well. The opponents of euthanasia twitched and bit their fingernails. They could only hope for an easy letdown. Seconds passed while everyone waited for Macintosh to say something, anything.

Suddenly he slammed his file shut and leaned quickly forward with an energy no one in the room had yet seen. He was angry, livid in fact. This argument was more than disagreeable to him. It was despicable, and it touched a raw nerve with this disabled man.

"Senator Cousins," he began. "Let me get your argument straight."

"Of course." Cousins was taken aback by Macintosh's sudden aggressiveness, but was only too happy to have his argument restated before all these people, even if it was by someone in very poor spirits.

Fundamental issue: Are moral questions to be decided by popular opinion?

"Are you telling us," Macintosh asked him, "that the way we in this society ought to decide what is right and wrong on the moral and social issues we face is by the polls, by a simple vote? Is this your basis, your method for deciding these issues?"

Cousins was unhappy with this portrayal of his argument. He frowned and said, "Oh, I'm not sure. I suppose you could put it that way."

"Does that mean yes?" Macintosh probed.

"Yes, I guess it does. All I'm saying is that we should ask the people what they think."

"And we should do this by looking at the polls? Is that it? That was your purpose in listing all those polls wasn't it?"

"Yes," Cousins admitted.

Macintosh looked down at the notes he had scribbled while Cousins had been speaking. "And then we should make our decision, cast our vote according to what these polls say?" he said. "Isn't that your method? After all, it's the people's country, not ours, and we should be willing to live with whatever decision they have already made. That

FINAL WISHES ─────────────────────────── 177

is what you said, is it not?" Macintosh looked up from his note pad and waited.

It took Cousins a second or two to look directly at Macintosh's face, but he had no choice but to agree. Macintosh had parroted his very words back to him. He finally nodded and said crisply, "Yes, that is what I said."

Macintosh shook his head, growing even angrier. "I have to tell you, Senator, that I find that incredibly short-sighted and tragically ill-informed."

Cousins shifted uncomfortably in his chair. "You are entitled to your opinion, sir."

"That is my opinion," Macintosh replied, "and I hold it because I've read history."

"History?" Cousins looked surprised.

"Yes, history. And I sometimes wonder if we have learned anything from it." His voice was rising.

Cousins shrugged and raised his hands in the air again. "I'm afraid I have no idea what you're getting at, sir."

Macintosh bristled. "And that is exactly the problem, Senator. One hundred and fifty years ago, in most Western democracies, a majority of citizens were opposed to women voting." (a) Implications of this principle if true

Cousins flinched as he suddenly thought of the implications of this for his argument. (1) Women and the vote

"Does this mean," Macintosh continued, "that at that time, it was right and good that women were not permitted to vote? And would you say that it was right specifically because the polls would have registered a majority against it? Are you willing to say that, Senator?"

People had quit laughing and the mood had turned somber. Macintosh was rubbing the senator's face in an extremely volatile issue and had placed him squarely on the wrong side of that issue, and every single person in the room knew it. But he was not finished yet. He had another fact from history, a much harder-hitting one for this senator to chew on. In fact, for a fleeting moment, he had considered not using it; it seemed too dangerous. In the end, he shelved his caution, deciding that if anyone deserved to have his nose rubbed in this fact, it was this senator, right now.

(2) Slavery   "There was also a time in our country," he declared very deliberately, "not too long ago when a majority of citizens also believed it was good and right for black people to be regarded as property and used as slaves."

Cousins eyes closed and his head turned downward. He slowly exhaled a very large breath, and his mind began to race in search of a response.

"The polls would have registered majority support for that practice," Macintosh thundered. "In fact, as you know, Senator, a large part of the economy had become dependent upon it, and whenever slavery was attacked by its opponents, the defenders of the abominable practice predicted dire consequences that were sure to follow if it was abolished."

Macintosh had grown passionate. "Are you seriously telling us that because the majority supported the practice of slavery it was good and right, at that time, to round up black people in Africa, herd them into stench-filled ships, transport them to another country, sell as property those who survived the hellish trip over, and treat them as such for the rest of their lives?"

Cousins's face was crimson, and he shook with anger. "This is preposterous!" he roared, jumping up from his chair and pointing at Macintosh. "Mr. Moderator, this man is implying that because I favor legalizing physician-assisted suicide, I must also favor slavery! This is absurd and offensive, and I resent the implication!"

Every person in the room froze instantly in a state of shock. The silence was immediately followed by a widespread, spontaneous burst of emotion as people began to shout, boo and point fingers toward the front of the room. Some spewed out vile insults at Macintosh for implying that Cousins supported slavery. Others, who were convinced by Macintosh, threw derogatory comments at Cousins. The room had turned to bedlam within five seconds.

Macintosh looked at the ceiling and rolled his eyes. He was bewildered by this outburst and had no idea what should happen next. Senator Ryan began pounding his gavel furiously in an effort to regain control. He gave a nod to a tall man wearing a suit and a small earpiece, and instantly members of the security force took up strategic positions throughout the room. A few were talking into portable radios and cellular phones. One was forced to usher a particularly incensed man out a side door.

The force of their presence had its effect, and in less than a minute the bedlam had subsided. Ryan asked Cousins to take his seat and then pled with the audience for order. He managed to remind them twice that the hearings were almost over.

Turning to Macintosh, he said sternly, "If you have something left to say, I suggest you make it concise so we can adjourn these hearings while there is still some order. I would also caution you," he added, leaning forward and holding up both index fingers for emphasis, "to avoid inflammatory language, please. You are close to the edge." He was not smiling.

Macintosh breathed deeply. Anything he said would only inflame a highly volatile situation. On the other hand, Cousins and his argument were so pernicious to him that he simply didn't care if Cousins found his comments offensive. Eventually he leaned toward his microphone again. "I'm disappointed, Senator," he said.

"None of us is doing cartwheels right now, Mr. Macintosh," Ryan replied dryly. "What exactly disappoints you?"

"The fact that the senator has entirely missed the point about slavery," Macintosh replied.

"And what is the point he missed?" Ryan asked, temporarily speaking for Cousins, who was in no condition to continue the dialogue just yet.

"It is that if we are to decide morality by looking at the polls, as he has argued, then we will have no choice but to admit that slavery in the United States was at one time morally justified. After all, a majority favored it."

Cousins shook his head slowly and gave Macintosh a look that would have melted rubber. Macintosh looked back at him and then spoke again with a touch of cynicism that he found impossible to suppress.

"After all, Senator," he said, "last time I checked, the country was a democracy during the days of slavery too." The sound of people booing penetrated the silence again. Cousins bristled.

Macintosh plowed ahead. "Didn't the people at that time have a right to choose their own fate on matters of moral and social policy? Isn't that what the senator said?" Ryan nearly cut him off.

"Surely a minority has no right to impose its views about such matters on the majority," Macintosh continued, his voice now dripping with sarcasm. "I guess that means that because a majority of citizens supported this treatment of black people, then it was good and right at that time, wasn't it?"

"Mr. Macintosh, I caution you!" Ryan cut in.

Macintosh paused, nodded toward Senator Ryan and then looked at Cousins angrily. "I think not!" He drew out the words one at a time.

"But Mr. Macintosh," Ryan interjected. "To be fair to the senator, he has just told us that he does *not* believe slavery was good or right. Indeed, I know from years of experience of working with Senator Cousins that he does not believe it was anything but a shameful blight on our national history."

Macintosh smiled. "I know," he said, "and that is my point exactly."

Ryan looked surprised. "*What* is your point?"

"That although the senator believes slavery is a great evil and that it should not have been practiced in this country, the fact is that by his way of deciding moral questions, slavery *is* morally justified, whether he likes it or not."

"His way?" Ryan asked.

"Yes. His way is to look at the polls and vote that way. (b) Popular
Since the senator does *not* agree that slavery was morally opinion: not a
justified at that time, even though the majority favored it, reliable guide
he should drop his way of deciding moral questions. He moral issues
should admit that looking at the polls does not always lead
to truth on moral questions. He has already admitted it for
the issue of slavery."

Cousins was now subdued and sat at the table scowling
contemptuously at this man who had done what he had
thought no one would do. He had argued against his democratic principle. Suddenly he realized the disabled man was
speaking again and was addressing his comments to him.

"People like you scare me, Senator," Macintosh was
saying. "You have heard arguments this week that legalizing physician-assisted suicide will impose a devastating
burden on the entire class of the elderly, terminally ill,
and disabled, and that it will lead us down a slippery slope
to other abuses. Furthermore, it will open up the possibility that misdiagnosed patients who are not even seriously
ill will receive assisted suicides. Are you really willing to
ignore all of this and to legalize the practice, simply
because the risk is only to minority groups and the polls
indicate majority support for the practice?"

It was obvious that Cousins did not care to respond further to anything Macintosh said. There was a long pause
during which Ryan looked back and forth at his colleagues, whispering and nodding. Suddenly Macintosh
spoke up again. "Senator Ryan," he called out.

Ryan looked up, surprised to hear from him. "Yes, Mr.
Macintosh?"

"With your permission," he said, "there is one further
observation I would like to make about the polls the senator spoke of, if I may."

Ryan looked down the row of his colleagues, then
asked, "Is this really necessary?"

"Yes, I believe so. It is information necessary for understanding these polls," he replied.

Ryan inhaled deeply then slowly let the air out. "Go

ahead," he assented, after extracting a guarantee that it would not take more than five minutes.

"Thank you, Senator," Macintosh replied. He turned very deliberately in his chair to face Cousins. "You and I both know," he said to him, "that poll results vary. It all depends upon how the question is worded and on how well-informed the respondents are. Have you never had reason to be leery about a poll result, Senator?"

Cousins was still bristling but reached for his microphone and spoke in an intense but controlled voice. "These are reputable polling firms, Mr. Macintosh. Gallup, Harris, CNN, *Time, Macleans,* Decima. I'm sure you won't question their ability to conduct a reliable poll."

Then he paused and cleared his throat. "Sure, I've questioned poll results," he said adamantly, "but only when there was a problem with the question, not simply because I did not like the results."

"Exactly," said Macintosh. "Sometimes there is a problem with the question, and when there is, we have a right to be suspicious about the results."

"And?" Cousins moved his hand in outward circles. "How is that relevant to these polls conducted by these reliable firms, Mr. Macintosh?"

(c) Popular opinion polls must be read with care.

"It is relevant because polls on euthanasia are especially suspect. We should question them even more than we do other polls."

"And why is that?"

"Because although according to the polls, it almost always looks like there is strong support for legalizing euthanasia, voters rarely go that way when given a chance in an actual vote or referendum. They start high and end low."

"What starts high?"

"Support for euthanasia. When people are asked for a simple yes or no to euthanasia, the numbers in favor are always high. That is because no one is actually casting a vote or making a decision on anything."

"Uh-huh. And you're telling us that the number of people who support it drops when people have to actually cast a vote in a referendum on this issue?"

"Exactly. As people become more informed and have to cast an actual vote on the matter, support for euthanasia always drops until, in the end, these referenda have virtually always failed. Remember Washington in 1991 and California in 1992? Both voted against it in a referendum. So much for the strong majority in favor of legalization."

(1) Poll results change when people become informed about the subject.

Cousins smiled. "Are you forgetting Oregon in 1997? It passed there, you know."

Macintosh nodded. "Yes, it did, and I did not say it *never* passes. I said it usually fails, which is true. It shows that the overwhelming support by the people you spoke of earlier is simply not there when people are actually called on to make a decision on this issue."

"But there is more," Macintosh said, looking down at his file. "I wonder how much we can really learn in the first place about people's views on euthanasia by only asking a simple question."

Cousins shrugged.

"You see, it all depends on people's understanding of the term *euthanasia*."

(2) Poll results change when questions are phrased differently.

"Are you saying that people don't know what this words means, Mr. Macintosh? Isn't that a little paternalistic?"

"It would be, but I'm not saying that."

"What then?"

"I'm saying that different people mean different things when they use words like this."

"What things?" Cousins pressed.

"I know of one survey," Macintosh replied, "which, as expected, found a small majority in favor of legalizing euthanasia."

Cousins raised his hands. "There you go."

"But these pollsters went further. They asked more questions to try to find out exactly what people *understood* by the term *euthanasia*. You see, if you and I mean different things by the term, then we are saying different things when we both answer yes to the same question, are we not?"

"I suppose."

"So do I. To make a long story short," Macintosh elaborated, "they discovered that 67 percent of those who claimed to favor legalizing euthanasia were wrongly including in their definition of euthanasia the right to refuse medical treatment. The trouble is that this is not euthanasia and it is already legal and available anyway. What is more, a further question by the pollsters found that only 57 percent of all respondents even knew that refusing medical treatment was already legal.[1]

"So how many people were actually in favor of going that next step and giving doctors the right to actively end a patient's life through a lethal injection when the person would not otherwise die?"

Cousins shrugged. "It's your poll."

"No sir, it was not my poll, and the fact is, we don't know how many were in favor of moving to that next step, at least not from this poll. What we do know is that advocates of legalization point to polls like this all the time to 'prove' that the majority supports euthanasia."

The hearings were over. No other senators had further questions and Senator Ryan was in no mood to entertain more anyway. His closing comments were brief and concise. He thanked all participants, delegates, members of the audience and the security force. He assured the audience that he and his colleagues had their work cut out for them.

The full senate was to begin debating the issue in just over a week, and they would debate for five days. After that a vote would be taken on the senate floor. The gavel rapped and bedlam erupted. Ryan leaned back, wiped his brow with a handkerchief and said a prayer of thanks that at least this part of the process was behind them.

Reporters and TV camera crews rushed over to Macintosh, Ryan and Cousins with their myriad of questions. Before heading for the exit doors, Ron walked close to the front to get in on some of the action. He could overhear Cousins explaining his view of polls and surveys, and even of slavery. It was obvious that this last part annoyed him greatly, but he was subdued and controlled.

20

The Evergreen was dark, just as Becker had said. It was also filling up quickly with tired professionals stopping in for a few stiff shots before heading back to the suburbs. This was a place where realtors, bankers, brokers, senate staffers and others met to conduct business or just to unwind. It definitely was not as quiet as Ron had been led to believe, but he decided not to push the issue.

Ron arrived thirty minutes late due to the extra long hearings that day. He saw a large man dressed in casual pants and a T-shirt, holding a note pad. He introduced himself and they sat down at a table in the far corner. Becker was thirty years old and had worked for the *Springfield Sun* for three years, having come from a small rural paper where he had cut his teeth.

He wore dark-rimmed glasses and had a short haircut. He was friendly and seemed a bit uneasy. They ordered Scotch on the rocks. Ron decided to take control of the discussion. After all, he had something Becker wanted, not the other way around.

"A few rules of the game," Ron said. "First, everything I say is on condition of confidentiality."

Becker shrugged as if he were willing to go along with this requirement but was disappointed by it.

"My name will not appear in any of your stories. If it appears at all, it will be only after the vote in the senate, and then only if they vote to legalize it. If the measure fails, my name will never appear."

"Can I assume from this that you are hoping the measure will pass?"

"No."

"Do you have any more rules?"

"Only that I will answer some questions for you, but not many. Of course I'll decide which ones to answer. I'm here only because I want you to get it right, OK? I will mainly confirm or deny what you have already heard."

Becker nodded. "I can live with that," he said dryly. "You said Dr. Patrick Metcalfe is a friend of yours."

"Yes."

"The same Dr. Patrick Metcalfe who is being featured on *ATN News*?"

"Yes."

"How long have you known him?"

"Twenty-six years. We were colleagues in medical school."

"Are you planning to assist him in ending his life?"

"Planning, no."

"Let me rephrase that. Are you *considering* helping him end his life?"

"He's asked me to help him, yes."

"So you are the mystery physician ATN has been speaking of over the past few days?"

"Yes." Becker took a deep breath and exhaled slowly as he scribbled furiously, savoring this incredible fact that no other news source had been able to discover. It was a true exclusive, and he could barely conceal his smile. He envisioned the headlines.

"Have you made up your mind whether you will assist Dr. Metcalfe in dying?" This was a thinly disguised repeat of the question he had asked a few moments before.

"No, I have not."

"In general terms, then," Becker persisted, searching for some way to get an answer to this question, "would a physician in your circumstances be well advised to agree to a request like this?"

Ron smiled. "Nice try."

Becker grinned sheepishly and moved on, probing Ron for another fifteen minutes or so about Pat's reasons for wanting to die, about Ron's reasons for either helping him or not, and about what this might do to Ron's future practice and career.

Ron answered most of the questions but gave few details. He corrected a few misconceptions and took a moment to explain Dr. LeRoy Grange's contention that legalizing physician-assisted suicide would impose a devastating burden on all people who are elderly, terminally ill or disabled. He made sure Becker knew that the hospice movement opposed legalizing physician-assisted suicide. Apart from that, he said little about reasons and arguments.

After the interview, Becker asked Ron if he could call him again. Ron said yes but would not guarantee any more meetings.

21

Ron was packing his suitcase the next morning in his room at the Hilton when the phone rang. He answered, and the caller identified herself as the receptionist at the medical offices of Doctors Metcalfe, Johnson and Green in Chicago. Her name was Rita Doell, and she was polite but deadly serious. It took Ron a few seconds to realize that this was the office of Dr. Patrick Metcalfe, the man who was the reason he was here.

"You don't know me," she said, "but Dr. Metcalfe gave me your name and phone number."

"Yes," Ron replied, nervously. Why would Patrick be passing out this information to his receptionist?

"He speaks very highly of you, Dr. Grey," she continued.

"Thank you," Ron replied hesitantly.

"I'm afraid I have some bad news," Rita said soberly.

Ron's mind began to whirl as he quickly ran through all the possibilities he could think of. "Bad news?" he repeated, suddenly feeling very queasy.

"Yes. It's about Dr. Metcalfe."

What now? Ron wondered.

"His condition has worsened much faster than expected. Test results came in this week and it appears he's had the disease quite a while longer than anyone knew. Probably six to eight months. In the past week it has moved into another stage and advanced quickly."

Ron leaned on the table for strength. His knees felt wobbly and weak. "Is that all?"

"I wish it were, sir."

Ron cringed. "What else?"

"There is one more thing," she continued. "Yesterday he had a fall, here at the office. He was just walking down the hall and he lost his balance. His strength just disappeared. He had not been steady all morning. Anyone could see that, and I should have said something earlier. I feel dreadful." Her voice trailed off.

Ron swallowed hard, his stomach in knots, as he struggled to maintain his composure. The thought of his long-time friend lying on the floor, helpless, in pain and probably embarrassed, stricken with a hellish disease, was more than he could take. Tears trickled down his face.

Why? he felt like shouting. And why *Patrick?* What had this hard-working physician, who loved his patients, and his family even more, ever done to deserve such an ending? He thought of the scoundrels and criminals out there who seemed to skate through life with hardly a hint of suffering. Why do good people suffer while wicked people prosper?

No wonder Pat wanted to end it all his way, on his terms, at his time. Who could blame him? At least that way he could look death in the face and have the last laugh. He would get *it* before *it* got *him.*

Suddenly the world seemed like a crazy place to Ron. It made no sense. Where was the justice? The fairness? Could anyone hope to find these elusive jewels here on this planet?

Then he heard the sound of Rita's voice again. "Dr. Grey," she was saying. "Are you still there?"

"Yes," he whispered and then asked, "When did this happen?"

"Two days ago, on Tuesday afternoon. Dr. Green accompanied him home that day, and Dr. Metcalfe has not been back since. He had only been working four hours a day, and we all knew it wouldn't be long."

"Yes, he told me."

"Since his fall, it's become clear that he is unable to continue working at all."

"Uh-huh." Ron knew it had to happen sometime.

"ATN did another interview with him as well."

Ron was floored. "You're kidding!"

"Afraid not. He called in yesterday when it was all over, and we talked for fifteen minutes. They asked questions about him quitting work and went on at length about his fall at the office once he mentioned that. Pat said it was a hard interview. They had to shut it down three times."

Ron shook his head in disbelief and hung up the phone. He fell onto the bed and stared at the ceiling. "Patrick, Patrick," he whispered. "Why you?" He knew there was no good answer to that question.

He grabbed the phone again and punched in his home phone number. Judy was on the line within seconds, and he told her everything. The advancement in Patrick's illness, his fall, and the fact that Ron couldn't blame him for wanting to die on his own terms.

Judy listened to it all and simply asked, "So what are you going to do?"

"What do you mean, what am I going to do?"

"You went out there with a big decision to make. What are you going to do?"

Judy had never been known for an evasive, softball approach to life, and at this moment she was acting true to character.

"I really don't know," Ron said almost with embarrassment.

"Ron! Ron!" she said slowly, with deep feeling.

"I'm struggling, Judy. I know Patrick wants me to help him die, and if anyone deserves to get something they want right now, it's Pat."

"Well then?"

"But he's my friend." Ron's voice rose with passion. "How can I help him die? I didn't go to medical school to help people die."

Judy listened quietly and then said, "You asked me a

question last time we talked."

"That's right, I did," Ron agreed. "Do you have an answer?"

"Yes."

Ron waited, surprised by the suspense of the moment. After all, this was only one opinion from one person, but somehow he knew it was an opinion that would matter greatly.

"I've spent the past two days putting myself in Jean's shoes," Judy said, softly.

"Uh-huh."

"If you were the one dying and considering a physician-assisted suicide," Judy continued, "it would tear my guts out. I can't even describe the pain I would feel."

"Yes," Ron responded impatiently, wishing she would get to her answer. He had thought about his question to her ever since he had asked her, and he had realized that he really had no idea how she would respond. And then it came.

"I wouldn't want to lose you," she said, in a voice barely above a whisper. "Not one day sooner than I had to. And I'm telling you now, Ron, that I wouldn't want you to end your life."

Ron listened, mesmerized by what he was hearing.

"You can call me selfish if you want but I wouldn't want to lose you," she said again.

"But what about me and my pain?" Ron pleaded. "If I was dying, what if I *wanted* to die, like Patrick does?"

"You didn't ask me that," Judy replied firmly. "I can't control what you might feel or want. You asked me what I would want, and I'm telling you. I wouldn't want you to suffer pain. I would want you to be comfortable, and I would do everything I could to make life better for you, but I wouldn't want you to do it. I mean it, Ron. You asked me a question and that is my answer."

Ron breathed in deeply and slowly exhaled. He, too, would need an answer—for Pat—in the very near future.

"I love you, Judy!" he responded. "It's been too long. The

world may be a crazy place, but at least I've got you."

"I love you too, Ron."

***

Ron's next meeting with Pat would be difficult and tense, and he decided to postpone it until the following day. His plan was to arrive at Pat and Jean's home on Friday and fly home on Sunday. After that there was no plan except going back to work—and of course making the hardest decision of his life.

Would he be coming back to Chicago? He didn't know. If he did, would it be to administer the final injection to his friend Pat? The very thought made him nauseous and dizzy.

Picking up the phone a third time, he called Pat. Their conversation was emotional and hard on both of them. Thanks to his fall at the office, he now had a bruised elbow and a large bump on his head. "It wasn't pretty," he had informed Ron, sounding more despondent than Ron had ever heard him.

He was actually doing somewhat better physically. He felt steadier and stronger, but his self-confidence had taken a hit. "I never know from one hour to the next what kind of shape I'll be in," he told Ron. "One moment I'm steady and strong. The next, I drop something for no apparent reason." The disease was advancing on him and would continue to take away everything that gave him happiness in life. His voice had drifted off as he said these words.

Conspicuously missing in their conversation was anything about Pat's wish that Ron would help him die. But the issue was there, lurking behind everything that was said, and they both knew it. Each waited for the other to raise it, and since no one did, it didn't come up. It would be the next big item for discussion. It was what Ron had to look forward to when he arrived at Pat's.

22

R on's knock on the door was gentle. It was 11:30 on Friday morning, and the sun warmed the gentle, rippling breeze, making the day the first good one of the spring to be outside. Someone cracked the door, then opened it. Pat was leaning on the doorknob with one hand.

"Ron!" he said with emotion, grabbing the back of Ron's neck in a hard embrace. He let go of the door, bumping into it, causing it to bang into the wall. A hanging key rack clanged to the floor. The sudden clatter brought Jean hurriedly running to the door, the two Labradors following. Her hand was over her mouth as she rounded the corner, expecting the worst. Seeing Ron and Pat, she stopped in her tracks, then slowly walked toward Ron. "Thank you!" she whispered as she, too, hugged him warmly.

The visit with Pat and Jean began better than Ron had expected. It was lunchtime when he arrived, and Jean had prepared an appetizing spread of garden salad, the homemade chowder that was her specialty, cheese bread, and coffee and cake for dessert.

Pat's worsening condition was obvious. Everything took more time and effort. Ron struggled with knowing when to assist him and risk hurting his pride, and when not to and appear to be uncaring.

After the meal they all took more coffee and sat outside on the deck. Beside them was an open lawn leading out to a group of trees that would soon fill out and provide Pat and Jean with privacy from their neighbors. Classical music played softly through the open windows.

They sipped coffee in silence for a few minutes. Ron searched for something significant and appropriate to say but came up short. Suddenly Pat's face broke into a smile and he started laughing. "Remember the time we sprayed the university president's Mercedes with spray paint and hid behind the trees to watch his reaction when he came? What a sight!"

Ron suddenly remembered and began to shake with laughter. "Yeah, I remember," he said between breaths. "It was washable paint, but he didn't know that. I thought he was going to have a cardiac arrest right then, the way he raced around looking for someone to blame."

"It was you, me and Jordan," Pat said, recalling another medical student who had later quit the program after a nasty fight with the administration. "Jordan was actually called in for an interrogation, but not a word. It was called the code of silence, and we had it mastered."

The stories continued and the laughter grew. Jean chuckled at the sight of two grown men laughing and chortling like boys. The one about the university president led to one about a new, young professor who they had decided needed to be brought down a notch or two from his ivory tower.

Jean shook her head. "Did you two do any actual *studying* while you were in medical school?" she asked. "I'm beginning to wonder."

"If you only knew," was the only answer she could extract from the two physicians. After a few more head-shaking stories, she finally excused herself and went inside the house.

Then Pat turned to Ron. "We don't have much time. What would you like to talk about?"

Ron was surprised. "You're asking *me?* I was about to ask you. The fact is my mind is full, and most of it is not very enjoyable stuff. It's not easy to have an enjoyable conversation at a time like this."

"We haven't done badly so far," Pat replied.

Ron had to agree, and then he asked, "What are *you*

thinking of? What's been going through your mind?"

Pat sat quietly then finally said, "Do you know what's the hardest?"

Ron shook his head.

"It's the waiting," Pat mumbled. "It's wondering what's coming next. It's getting out of bed every morning gingerly and cautiously, wondering if my legs will work today. It's knowing that each day brings me further deterioration and one day closer to my meeting with the grim reaper."

Ron winced.

"Some people die instantly," Pat continued, "in car wrecks, or gun fights, or wars, or firing lines or suicides." He looked up at Ron. There it was, the word *suicide*. It was on the table, waiting for Ron to pick it up and do something with it. But Pat spoke again.

"Not a bad idea, don't you think? No waiting. No wondering. Just take control and decide when you want the game to end."

Suddenly Ron wished more than ever before that he could talk his friend out of this. "C'mon Pat, don't do it! Life is not a game!"

"I can't help it."

"Please, Pat!"

"I've been thinking a lot about this, Ron. I've really beaten myself up over it."

"So have I, believe me," Ron answered.

Pat lowered his head and looked down at the table. "I look at you and I see a healthy, bright man, a physician, a husband and a father. You've got a future, Ron. I don't. Look at me and tell me to my face that I have a future."

Ron sat stone-faced, saying nothing.

"I look at you," Pat pushed on, "and wish I could be something different. I wish I could be you, but I can't. The only future I've got is further deterioration, more loss of whatever dignity I have left."

Ron bolted forward in his chair. "No! No! That's where you're wrong!"

Pat was taken aback. "Where?" he nearly shouted.

Does a debilitating disease destroy dignity?

Understanding
dignity

"You don't lose your dignity just because you lose control of your body," Ron replied passionately. He surprised himself by the conviction with which he spoke these words.

Pat leaned forward in his chair. "What are you saying, Ron?"

"I'm saying that dignity does not consist in having control. It's in the way we respond when we lose control. That's true dignity, and you can have it, Pat, even without having full control of your life!" He stopped and waited for Pat to answer.

"That's a new twist on an old word," Pat finally said.

They sat in silence for a few seconds until Pat spoke again. "I've got to do it for Jean," he said. "Why should she have to watch me and care for me as I waste away for who knows how long? This could go on for years."

Ron shook his head silently, and his mind raced to his phone conversation with Judy about that very idea. "So you're doing this for Jean?"

"Partly, yes."

Is PAS ever a
favor to loved
ones?

"Is that how *she* feels? Is this really a favor to her? Shall I call her out here right now and put it to her? Hey Jean, would Pat here be doing you a favor if he committed suicide so you wouldn't have to care for him any more or watch him die? Let's call her right now."

"C'mon, Ron."

Ron pressed further. "Is that how *you* would feel if it were the other way around?"

"That's entirely different!"

"Is it really? Have you ever thought about the guilt she might feel if she really believed you ended your life because you didn't want to be a burden to her?"

"Guilt?"

Could PAS
burden those
left behind
with guilt?

"Yes, old fashioned guilt. I can tell you this much. That's how most family members who are left behind by a victim of suicide feel, especially if the person tells them she did it because she didn't want to burden them anymore. They beat themselves up. As far as they're concerned, it's their fault the person is dead. They must have made her feel she was too much of a burden on them. Now they wish they could go back and tell her it wasn't so, but it's too late, and they live with their guilt day after day."

Pat got out of his chair and walked slowly to the edge of the patio. He leaned over the railing, studying the lawn below. Ron watched him and decided he should drop the issue for now.

Finally, Pat turned and looked across the deck, directly into Ron's eyes. "Are you telling me that you won't do it, Ron, that you won't help me end my life?"

Here it was, the moment Ron knew would be coming. He had prepared his answer but suddenly felt tongue-tied, like there was no good answer. Getting out of his chair, he eased over to the railing to stand near Pat, coffee in hand, and look out over the flower beds that Jean had freshly cultivated the day before.

"You're my close friend, Pat," he said, turning to look at him, "and I would do almost anything for you. You know that."

Pat did know it, but at this moment he sensed a different answer was coming.

"I'm telling you that I *can't* do it," Ron said. "I've been wrestling with this for days, believe me. It's been the toughest dilemma of my life, but I now know that I can't do it. Not for you or for anyone else. And I have to tell you, Pat, that I hope the senate does not legalize it."

Pat looked at the floor, shaking his head slowly. "I don't believe this," he said in a sad monotone, barely above a whisper. "Why not? All the law would be doing is giving a few suffering people the choice of ending their suffering with a doctor's help. It's their personal, private choice. What's the problem?" He walked slowly toward his chair.

"You've just said it," Ron replied, as gently as he could. "You've just nailed the problem."

Pat raised his hands and looked around blankly after he

slumped back into his chair. "What did I say?"

"You said the law would be doing nothing more than giving a few suffering people the choice to end their suffering."

"Yes, I did."

"But that's *not* all it would be doing." Ron paced along the deck, sliding his hand along the railing. "Legalizing physician-assisted suicide would do so much more than that. If that was all there were to it, I would be in favor of it."

"What are you talking about, Ron? What else would it do?"

Ron let out a huge breath and looked at Pat. Over the past week, he had thought about the answer to this very question almost nonstop. It was this idea, from Dr. Leroy Grange, which had first caused him to question physician-assisted suicide. He spoke slowly, choosing each word carefully. "If we legalize it, we will fundamentally change a public policy and that has consequences for many other people."

"Such as?"

"The elderly, terminally ill, and the disabled."

Pat was unfazed, almost defiant. "Yes," he responded, "We'd be giving all these people a choice to end their suffering if they wish. It would be their choice to end it or not. Somehow, I don't see a problem here."

Ron chuckled quietly. "I learned something about choices last week."

"Oh yeah?"

"I learned that not all choices are a favor to a person. Some choices can actually be burdens, like when political leaders are faced with the choice of sending young men and women into battle, knowing that if they do some will die, but if they don't other people will be raped and murdered and their homes pillaged. Haven't you ever said the words, 'now there's a choice I'm glad I don't have to make'? It's just too simplistic to say that we are always, invariably, doing people a favor by giving them choices."

Pat nodded silently and then said, "OK, you've got a

point there. But what burden are we possibly putting on people who are elderly, terminally ill or disabled by giving them the choice to end their lives?"

By this time, Ron had also settled back into his chair. "The burden of having to justify their own continued existence," he replied, softly. "And our timing would be horrible."

"Timing?"

"Yes. We'd be doing this to these people precisely at the time in their lives when they already feel useless, discouraged and a burden to others."

Pat sat quietly, mouthing those words as they ran through his mind.

"Along with the choice to die," Ron added, "comes the decision of whether one should live or die. You can't have one without the other. It is the unintended consequence, and it is devastatingly real to our most vulnerable people. They can be asked, and they will definitely ask themselves, why they should live on and continue to use up valuable medical resources and be a burden and expense to others when they no longer have to. Why shouldn't they just opt out of living? According to the palliative-care specialist I met with a few days ago, if the option of exiting the situation becomes legal and available, then the sense of obligation that people like this will feel to take this option will be overwhelming. You know what that means, don't you?"

Pat said nothing, so Ron answered. "It means that people will die out of a sense of duty to die even though, deep down, they would rather live."

"And that's why you're against this?" Pat asked.

"That's part of it. There's more. Legalizing physician-assisted suicide also creates the possibility of misdiagnosed patients who are not even seriously ill, but who think they are, asking for suicide assistance."

Pat closed his eyes and rubbed his forehead. This was obviously a new thought to him.

"You and I both know that medicine is not an exact science," Ron continued. "Misdiagnoses happen."

"That's true," Pat acknowledged.

"We also know that when people are informed by their doctors that they are terminally ill, they are extremely vulnerable at that point. Many become suicidal. As far as I'm concerned, people like this are in plenty of danger without us making it easier for them to make the biggest mistake of their lives."

Pat sucked in a huge breath and slowly exhaled it. "Wow!" he muttered, almost to himself, shaking his head.

Ron looked at him, unsure of how to interpret his response. "But there's another problem," he pressed on.

"What now?"

"I just don't see how anyone could contain a practice like physician-assisted suicide."

"Contain it?"

"Yes, limit it to just those few suffering, dying people you spoke of earlier."

"Why should that be so hard?"

"Because when we legalize the practice, we are actually legalizing a principle that says that people who decide their suffering is too great and do not want to endure it any longer have the right to receive a physician-assisted suicide."

"Uh-huh."

"But if we do that, how could we prevent a depressed, suicidal person who is not even physically ill from receiving one? Or a depressed teenager?"

Pat's eyes grew intense. "C'mon, Ron. We would prevent it by putting up safeguards stating exactly who could and could not receive one."

Ron thought back to Grange and Vanzanten. "In safeguards we trust," he murmured.

Pat winced.

"You could try safeguards," Ron continued, "and they might even work for a while, but the very principle itself will make it impossible to enforce those safeguards for long. The principle says that suffering people themselves decide if their suffering is too great and if they want a physician-assisted suicide. That's the whole point of legalizing the practice. What will we tell the depressed, suicidal middle-aged woman or teenager when they come requesting this service? 'I'm sorry, Ma'am, or son, your suffering is not bad enough, or it's the wrong kind of suffering'? How can we tell them that? The very reason for legalizing physician-assisted suicide is to put the choice, the autonomy, into the hands of the suffering person."

Pat had by now picked up a pen and pad of paper, and was laboriously taking down a few notes as Ron spoke.

"Do you know what is really ironic?"

"What?" Pat asked, no longer sure he even wanted to know.

Ron leaned forward and folded his hands. "I am convinced," he said, his voice rich with intensity, "that legalizing the practice will discriminate against the very people we are supposedly helping."

Pat laughed.

"I mean it, Pat. This is one of the most important reasons why I can't help you. The advocates of physician-assisted suicide tell us over and over that it is for the elderly, the terminally ill and the disabled."

"Yes?"

"But this week, I heard a different story from a disabled man. It was a story I couldn't ignore. This man said that if the practice becomes legal, it will mean that when an elderly, terminally ill or disabled person becomes suicidal, we'll be ready to help the person die."

"Uh-huh."

"But get this. When a young, healthy, able-bodied person is similarly suicidal, our response will be entirely different." Ron threw his hands in the air. "Suicide prevention is what the healthy person will get from us. Remember, both people are suffering and want to die. But as the man in the wheelchair put it, we are judging one group as having so much to live for that we will do everything in our power to prevent their death, while we judge the other as having so little to live for that we will actually help them die."

Pat was listening carefully, processing Ron's distinction between the two groups.

Ron was growing animated as he spoke. "Legalizing physician-assisted suicide and placing our safeguards around it would mean that we no longer want to prevent all suicides, only some of them—namely those of people whose lives we have judged to be worth living. We will actually be ready to help the unhealthy people die. I can't ignore it, Pat. In my book, that's making a discriminatory value judgment regarding which lives are worth fighting for and which aren't, and I, for one, am not willing to go there."

They talked for hours. Ron told Pat more about the senate hearings, about the specific delegations and their arguments, about Academics for Social Justice, about Will Jones and Dr. LeRoy Grange and the palliative-care ward, and about Malcolm Macintosh, the disabled man who opposed legalizing physician-assisted suicide.

Then Ron leaned forward in his chair looking intently at Pat. "But all these arguments don't mean a thing if they are only theoretical," he pleaded. "I'm thinking about you—my friend. Not some theory. Pat, if you were healthy but depressed, so depressed that you wanted to kill yourself, I couldn't—I wouldn't let you. I care for you too much. I'd want a chance to work it through with you. To let you know that no matter how bad your situation, I *value* you, and that your life *is* worth living. The fact that you are *not* healthy doesn't change a thing for me. I still value you. Your life is still worth living. Your worth is not based on your health."

The bittersweet tears that forced their way from under Pat's eyelids were the result of the storm in his heart. Only tears could express his feeling of emptiness and isolation caused by Ron's stalwart resolve. And only those same tears could express Pat's wonder and appreciation at Ron's unrelenting friendship and love.

Ron and Pat pulled out old photo albums and talked about easier times and about children and family. They drank Jean's new blend of coffee and watched the dogs play by the lake.

23

Ron's reunion with Judy on Sunday afternoon was glorious. As he walked off the plane back in Winnipeg, it seemed as if he had been gone for two months rather than ten days. So much had happened. She was waiting as he knew she would be, and looking even better than he had imagined.

He lifted her right off the ground in a hug and momentarily forgot about the emotional roller coaster he had been on, the facts and arguments he had been mulling over, and the decision he still had to make. At that moment, it was all gone. The feel of her body against his was nicer than anything he had felt for the previous two weeks. Judy always had a way of transporting him out of whatever was dragging him down and giving him a new enjoyment in life, and he loved her for it.

They loaded the luggage into the back of the Explorer and drove out of the airport parking area. "Where to?" Judy asked. "How about chicken and ribs?"

Ron looked over at her with a twinkle in his eye. "Personally, I had some place else in mind where I want to take you right now."

Judy looked at him out of the corner of her eye, smiling invitingly. "Hey Doctor, would you care to expand on that?"

"When was the last time I told you how beautiful you are?" he asked.

"About ten minutes ago."

"Ten minutes! I'll try not to let that happen again. And

just to make sure that I don't get out of practice, let's head home right away."

***

That day the *Chicago Tribune* carried a front page story about the Illinois state senate debates on physician-assisted suicide. Pat had immediately faxed it, and it was waiting at home when Ron and Judy arrived.

The story included a picture of the governor, who was said to be struggling with the issue but was so far standing by his plan not to veto any decision made by the senate.

There was also a photo of Senator Paul Ryan, the chair of the senate ethics committee, which had played the leading role in airing arguments and views on the issue. Ryan was now said to be leading the prolegalization forces. It was a gut-wrenching decision, he said, and yes, he had lost sleep over it.

"Of course there are dangers and risks," Ryan had explained. "I know that very well, but we must take those risks," he had stated adamantly to the reporter. "Our founding fathers took great risks to bring us our liberties, and we must continue to take risks to protect and even widen those liberties for those who are suffering and in need. We must also search diligently for ways to address and minimize those risks, but we must never sacrifice our liberties to avoid risks."

When pressed by the zealous reporter, Ryan admitted that his office was polling the voters of Illinois on a day-to-day basis. His decision, though, was not based on the polls. He was a man of conviction—a leader, not a follower.

Why the polls then? "They are routine," he insisted to the reporter. "It is simply a matter of being sensitive and responsive to the concerns of citizens. How can we respond to their concerns unless we know what they are?"

Ron shook his head and read on. At last count, the prolegalization forces in the senate were in the lead by a small margin of three votes, with all but eight senators having made up their minds on the issue. No one was predicting the final outcome just yet.

***

Ron arrived at the office at six o'clock on Monday morning to get a start on the mound of paperwork awaiting him before others would begin arriving. At half past seven he called Judy to tell her he had almost caught up and had surprised even himself at the speed with which it was done.

"Have you been listening to the news?" she asked.

"No, what?" he bolted upright.

"Two undecideds have come down in favor of legalization. I picked up the story on the radio. It's becoming a national story in both countries," she added.

Ron became dizzy. "I don't believe this," he whispered. "How can they?" He leaned back in his chair. "After the hearings? Weren't they listening? What were they thinking? Didn't they hear the same things I heard?"

"The news said the pressure on undecided senators has been overwhelming," Judy said. "Lobby groups from all over the country are there asking for meetings with every undecided senator. This gives the prolegalization side a five-vote lead, but it's not over yet. There are still six undecided senators as well as a couple of other soft yeses. It still could go either way."

Ron exhaled slowly and returned the receiver to its cradle.

***

It was six o'clock, time for the evening news, and Ron was anxious to hear what had happened in the senate debate. The Chicago station coming in on cable began with an exclusive story on the reasons behind the decision of the two undecided senators to come down on the side of legalization.

One of them, Senator Irene Landry, who was interviewed in front of the senate buildings, told about the impact on her of a recent visit by two victims of leukemia who wanted nothing more than the choice to end life gently and peacefully when they chose.

The TV cameras then panned across the well-kept grounds to Senator Paul Ryan, who was explaining the procedure of the vote. It would happen on Wednesday morning at eleven o'clock, and every senator was expected to be present for the crucial vote. He had struggled with issues before, he said, but never had the struggle been as deep and profound as this. "May God help us," he concluded, stepping away from the cluster of microphones bound together on the stand before him.

A throng of reporters then rushed in unison toward Ryan, yelling their questions all at once. But Ryan held up his hand, refusing to answer even one of them as he turned and strode away.

Then the scene changed to the office of a young ethics professor at the University of Chicago who was doing his best to concisely explain the issues surrounding physician-assisted suicide and what both sides would be arguing. This issue was so momentous, he said, because it touched on fundamental concerns like human suffering, personal rights, life and death, and the freedom of choice. The reporter seemed surprised to learn that the professor himself opposed legalizing the practice.

***

Ron arrived at work early again on Tuesday morning to be alone and enjoy the quietness of the office for an hour or so. After brewing the coffee again, he took a fresh cup outside and stared at the early-morning traffic as the city was coming to life. He sipped in silence. One more day, he told himself, then the big vote. He had already instructed Ruby to keep his schedule free from 10:30 to 11:30 on Wednesday morning. He would be alone in his office watching the vote.

***

The anchorwoman on the Tuesday evening news led off by announcing that there had been a dramatic change in the senate positions on physician-assisted suicide. The forces in favor of legalization had lost significant ground overnight and now held a slim, one-vote margin. Then came the explanation. Four more undecided senators had made up their minds to oppose legalization, and now only two senators remained undecided.

The scene immediately moved to the senate buildings in Springfield, where a group of reporters stood with a serious-looking Senator Paul Ryan. "We're down to the wire, and it's close, close, close," Ryan declared grimly.

He solemnly answered a few questions from the reporters and said things were right on schedule. Barring any unforeseen surprises, the vote would go ahead the next day, Wednesday, at eleven o'clock in the morning as planned. The issue had been divisive, he declared, and had obviously stimulated a great outpouring of emotion. He said that he hoped all citizens would unite around whatever decision was made by the highly contemplative body, and he professed great confidence in its collective wisdom.

24

At half past ten on Wednesday morning Ron slipped into his office, coffee in hand, and shut the door. Leaning back in his chair, he put his feet up on his desk and picked up the remote control. The same anchorwoman was on again, this time with two experts, one a lawyer and the other an ethics professor from a local university. As the hour went on, they were giving everything from the history of the debate surrounding physician-assisted suicide to interpretations of statements made by various people.

The professor briefly outlined the main arguments that both sides had used over the past two months and explained what made the issue so emotional and pressing. It touches on so many core, fundamental concerns, he said. The lawyer then outlined the legal process that was being followed, the purpose of the previous week's senate hearings, the role of the senate ethics committee and the influential position of Senator Paul Ryan as the chair of the committee.

Then the scene shifted to the senate buildings, and Ron sucked in his breath as he saw the crowds. There were a couple of hundred people in wheelchairs alone. A group of priests and nuns were standing quietly, as were many families with small children. The camera moved in closely on a group of people who were sitting on the grass and singing softly with their heads turned upward and their eyes closed. Another group might as well have been at a party. They wore baseball caps and had brought coolers, lawn chairs, mini-barbecues and Frisbees, which they were tossing back and forth on the outer edges of the senate grounds.

Banners bearing the words, "Doctors Are for Healing, Not Killing!" were being waved in one area, while other banners a few yards away proclaimed, "Death with Dignity."

Ron had no interest in watching the carnival that the place had become. Pushing the mute button, he sat back and sipped his coffee, waiting for the real action to begin. He looked at the phone and thought about what he would say to Pat in a few minutes. *Who will call first?* he wondered.

Ron thought about the two undecided senators and realized that in a sense the whole issue rested in their hands. *No pressure there,* he thought, chuckling, especially with a hundred delegations pulling at you to come their way and the world watching as you make your decision.

He walked to the window and thought of Pat, who he knew would be at home that very minute, glued to his television just as Ron was. Suddenly Ron glanced up at the silent television and saw the words plastered across the screen in large print: "Senate Vote In." He checked his watch. It was 11:15.

Lunging for the remote, Ron hit the volume button. An announcer was declaring that the vote had, indeed, been conducted, and they were all waiting for the official results. Unofficial results were swirling around, he said, but they were waiting for the official word before making their announcement. He spoke with an air of great urgency and importance, as though this were a defining historical moment for the nation, indeed for the world.

Suddenly there it was. "We now have the official result," declared the reporter. Then reaching for his earpiece, he tilted his head, paused for a second and announced the result. "The measure has failed!" he declared, excitedly, "By one vote! Physician-assisted suicide remains illegal in the state of Illinois."

The reporter went on to explain that the two undecided senators had both voted to oppose legalization, putting that side over the top by the slimmest of margins. Ron's eyes were stuck to the television. He was in a hypnotic trance. He didn't know what to feel.

Then the camera panned across the crowded lawn where the hushed crowd stood in anxious anticipation. At that moment, news of the vote was slowly spreading through the crowd as those with radios passed it on to others nearby.

The quiet was being replaced by pandemonium with some people jumping up and down, hugging one another and shouting for joy. Others were crying out in anger, upset at the "injustice."

"We won! We won!" one elated woman shouted at the top of her lungs.

"Who won?" a couple of others, a short distance away asked, looking bewildered and not having a clue whether to rejoice or cry.

The camera moved in on one man who was visibly sickened by the news and was being helped away by friends.

Ron grabbed the remote once again and shut the television off. He knew that at that precise moment his long-time friend would be tormented. He began to cry. He rubbed his eyes and cried for Pat and for the life he had been handed in the last six months. A life that had brought him so low that he would look upon news that he could not get help to take his own life as bad news.

Suddenly the phone rang. Ron picked it up cautiously but couldn't answer.

"Ron?" came the voice on the other end. It was Pat.

"Well, it didn't happen," Ron said slowly. "I suppose this changes things for you."

"I still need your help," Pat's words seemed dry, yet at the same time pleading.

Ron froze. Tears continued to stream down his face as he listened to his friend still asking him to help him die.

Eventually he spoke. "I love you, Pat, but I can't do it."

He could only imagine what Pat was feeling on the other end. Dying. Feeling so low that his main wish in life had become that a friend would help him die before his hellish disease worked its full ravages on him. Then being turned down by that friend. How much worse could life get than this?

"I'm sorry, Pat."

***

Pat's condition continued to worsen. He grew increasingly weak in his legs and shoulders. Four months later he became unable to walk without the assistance of a brace and a cane, and his speech was growing noticeably poorer.

Six months after that, Pat spoke only with great difficulty and had become confined to a wheelchair, which had been provided for him by the medical practice of Doctors Johnson, Green and Faulkner. Dr. Faulkner, a recent graduate from medical school, had joined Pat's old practice two months earlier. ATN continued to interview Pat and Jean, duly recording all changes in Pat's condition.

Six months after becoming wheelchair bound, on a cool day in August, Dr. Patrick Metcalfe gathered his wife and children, one surviving sister and a few of his closest friends to his bedside. An unnamed physician was also there. At the signal, given by Patrick, the physician administered lethal doses of Midazolam, Pancuronium and Phenobarbital. Antinausea drugs were administered first to prevent vomiting from the large doses of medication.

Dr. Ron Grey was among those invited. He declined the invitation but sent his warmest regards and deepest sympathies to Pat, Jean and their children. Scott Becker, Julia Benthall and Fritz Mahoney all asked to attend, but their requests were denied by Jean Metcalfe.

ATN edited all the interviews into a two-part documentary that aired on two consecutive Sunday evenings a couple of months after Pat's death. It was well advertised and attracted a huge viewing audience.

Notes

Chapter 4

[1]Dr. Willard Johnson, a Vancouver physician involved in the euthanasia debate, made this argument to me in a conversation.

[2]The argument that there is no meaningful moral distinction between killing and letting die in similar circumstances is made forcefully by James Rachels in "Euthanasia, Killing, and Letting Die," in *Ethical Issues Relating to Life and Death*, ed. John Ladd (Oxford: Oxford University Press, 1979), pp. 146-61. In this article, Rachels introduces his famous "Smith and Jones" example to illustrate that killing and letting die are equally reprehensible if the surrounding circumstances are the same. Furthermore, Peter Singer argues in *Rethinking Life and Death* (New York: St. Martin's, 1994), pp. 155-56, that patients would very likely benefit if the distinction between killing and letting die were dropped. A well-known response to Rachels has been made by Thomas D. Sullivan in "Active and Passive Euthanasia: An Impertinent Distinction?" *Human Life Review* 3, no. 3 (1977): 40-46. Two other critiques of Rachels's position are made by J. P. Moreland in "James Rachels and the Active Euthanasia Debate," reprinted in *Do the Right Thing*, ed. Francis J. Beckwith (Sudbury, Mass.: Jones and Bartlett, 1996), pp. 239-46, and by Tom L. Beauchamp in "A Reply to Rachels on Active and Passive Euthanasia," reprinted in *Contemporary Moral Problems*, ed. James E. White (New York: West, 1991), pp. 107-15.

Chapter 6

[1]Hodge's argument here, that the right to personal autonomy requires the legalization of PAS, is possibly the most common and fundamental contention supporting PAS. My experience has been that even when supporters of PAS are willing to concede numerous other points in this debate, they will continue to insist that the right to individual autonomy requires that people should be given the choice to die if they want it. For an analysis of the meaning of individual autonomy in society, see philosopher and lawyer John Warwick Montgomery, "Human Dignity in Birth and Death: A Question of Values," *Christian Legal Journal* 2, no. 3 (1993): 17-23. He argues that the very fact that each individual has the same inherent worth as each other individual creates a built-in restraint on our choices and actions. He applies this principle to a number of issues, including suicide. See Ronald Dworkin, *Life's Dominion: An Argument about Abortion, Euthanasia and Individual Freedom* (New York: Vantage Books, 1994), for a fuller statement of the argument from autonomy in favor of assisted suicide. This argument is also made by Russel Ogden in "The Right to Die: A Policy Proposal for Euthanasia and Aid in Dying," *Canadian Public Policy* 20, no. 1 (1994): 2-3. For a critique of this argument see Paul Chamberlain, "Physician-Assisted Suicide: Should We or Shouldn't We?" *The Scholaris* 1, no. 4 (1995): 1-6.

[2]The argument made here by Hodge, that killing and letting die are morally equivalent if the circumstances are the same, was made in this form by Dr. Faye Girsh, executive director of the Hemlock Society, in a series of forums she and I held on university campuses in October 1997. For further reading on this argument, refer to endnote two of chapter four.

[3]The statement that a slippery slope is "neither predictable nor absolutely preventable"

was made by Faye Girsh during the previously mentioned forums on physician-assisted suicide. For the view that safeguards could effectively prevent a slippery slope see Peter Singer, *Practical Ethics* (Cambridge: Cambridge University Press, 1979), pp. 128-29, 140-46. Singer sets out a number of safeguards that have been suggested by voluntary euthanasia societies around the world. Patrick Nowell-Smith, in "The Right to Die," in *Contemporary Moral Issues,* ed. Wesley Cragg (Toronto: McGraw-Hill Ryerson, 1992), pp. 7-15, also argues that most serious abuses of legalizing PAS can be "all but eliminated" through proper safeguards. For an opposing view on the effectiveness of safeguards see Barry A. Bostrom, "Euthanasia in the Netherlands: A Model for the United States?" *Issues in Law & Medicine* 4, no. 4 (1989): 471-75. Pointing to the Netherlands as an example, Bostrom describes the changing guidelines from 1973 to 1986 to demonstrate that euthanasia has become more widely practiced and for different reasons than at first intended. For another critique of the effectiveness of safeguards, see Herbert Hendin, *Seduced by Death,* 2nd ed. (New York: W.W. Norton, 1998), p. 136. He argues that it is impossible to regulate PAS. In his words, "Virtually every guideline set up by the Dutch—a voluntary, well-considered, persistent request; intolerable suffering that cannot be relieved; consultation; and reporting of cases—has failed to protect patients or has been modified or violated."

Chapter 7
[1]This argument is made by Russel Ogden in "When the Sick Request Death: Palliative Care and Euthanasia—A Continuum of Care?" *Journal of Palliative Care* 10, no. 2 (1994): 82-85. In this article Ogden includes a few accounts of botched suicide attempts that he discovered in his research in the AIDS community. For a critique of the botched-suicide argument, see physician H. Robert Pankratz, "The Person in Community: An Examination of Euthanasia," pp. 16-17. This was part of a brief to the Canadian Senate Committee on Euthanasia and Assisted Suicide presented by Canadian Physicians For Life on August 29, 1994.

Chapter 9
[1]For a full treatment of euthanasia in the Netherlands see Hendin, *Seduced by Death,* especially pp. 65-149. His contention is that euthanasia is out of control in the Netherlands and is being practiced far more widely than initially intended. For more specific details about the present practice of euthanasia in the Netherlands, see P. J. van der Mass, J. J. M. van Delden and L. Pijnenborg, *Euthanasia and Other Medical Decisions Concerning the End of Life* (New York: Elsevier, 1992), commonly called the Remmelink Report. See also P. J. van der Mass et al., "Euthanasia, Physician-Assisted Suicide, and Other Medical Practices Involving the End of Life in the Netherlands, 1990-1995," *New England Journal of Medicine* 335, no. 22 (1996): 1699-1705 and G. van der Wal et al., "Evaluation of the Notification Procedure for Physician-Assisted Death in the Netherlands," *New England Journal of Medicine* 335, no. 22 (1996): 1706-11. These two articles summarize a more recent study, commissioned by the Dutch government, that was released in 1995. For a positive perspective of the practice of euthanasia in the Netherlands, see Peter Singer, *Rethinking Life and Death,* pp. 141-58.

Chapter 10
[1]See philosopher Margaret P. Battin, "Age-Rationing and the Distribution of Health Care:

Is There a Duty to Die?" in *The Moral Life*, eds. Steven Luper-Foy and Curtis Brown (Toronto: Harcourt Brace, 1992), pp. 313-24. In this article Battin assumes a Rawlsian basis for rights and obligations in society and asserts that on this basis, while individuals would not have their lives "discontinued" while in full health, people who are irreversibly ill or of advanced age would have no automatic right to medical care. She says that at a certain point in their illness or age there would be a "disenfranchisement from care and the expectation that it is time to die" (p. 323). Wesley J. Smith gives a helpful summary of the issue in his book *Forced Exit* (New York: Random House, 1997), pp. 163-79. He includes a quote from former Colorado governor Richard Lamm, who said that old people "have a duty to die and get out of the way" (p. 172). Furthermore, renowned legal scholar Yale Kamisar has suggested that if euthanasia were adopted as general practice it could lead to a form of social coercion. In his words, "In a suicide-permissive society, in a climate in which suicide is the 'rational' thing *to* do, or at least a 'reasonable' option, will it become the unreasonable thing *not* to do? The noble thing *to* do? In a society unsympathetic to justifying an impaired or dependent existence, a psychological burden may be placed on those who do not think their illness or infirmity is reason for dying. The presence of a socially approved option becomes a subtle pressure to request it" (cited in Hendin, *Seduced by Death*, p. 214).

[2]This is a well known view of Dr. Jack Kevorkian, outspoken American advocate and practitioner of assisted suicide.

[3]This statement was made to me in a personal conversation in 1995 with Dr. Peter Kyne, a neuropsychiatrist and palliative-care expert in Vancouver, British Columbia. Yale Kamisar also says that if euthanasia became a socially approved option, there could be "subtle pressure to request it" (in Hendin, *Seduced by Death*, p. 214). See also *When Death Is Sought*, a study carried out and published by The New York State Task Force on Life and the Law, convened by governor Mario Cuomo, published in May 1994. The unanimous recommendations of the task force were that New York laws prohibiting assisted suicide and euthanasia should not be changed. One of the reasons given was that these practices "would be profoundly dangerous for many individuals who are ill and vulnerable." According to the task force, the "risks would be most severe for those who are elderly, poor, socially disadvantaged, or without access to good medical care" (p. ix).

[4]Bostrom, Barry A. "Euthanasia in the Netherlands: A Model for the United States?" *Issues in Law & Medicine* 4 (1989): 477-79. See also Hendin, *Seduced by Death*, pp. 124-41.

[5]This question was repeatedly put to audiences by Dr. Faye Girsh at the previously mentioned forums on PAS.

[6]A letter with the same import appeared in the *Vancouver Sun*, December 31, 1994.

Chapter 12

[1]Dr. Herbert Hendin, director of The American Foundation for Suicide Prevention, in the first edition of his book *Seduced by Death* (New York: W. W. Norton, 1997), p. 181, cites various studies to show that suicides are being committed today by people who mistakenly believe they have cancer. It is my contention that misdiagnoses lead to this type of mistaken belief about one's health.

[2]Hendin describes this "pressure for euthanasia from family and doctors" in *Seduced by Death*, 2nd ed., p. 213.

Chapter 13

[1]"Killing the Psychic Pain," *Time,* July 4, 1994, p. 55. This case was explored by Herbert Hendin, who traveled to the Netherlands and interviewed Dr. Chabot, the psychiatrist who administered the physician-assisted suicide. In *Seduced by Death,* 2nd ed., pp. 63-64, 76-87, Hedin provides a more complete description of the process leading to her death. See also Wesley Smith, *Forced Exit,* pp. 104-5, for another description of the case.

[2]See endnote three of chapter six for further readings on the question of the effectiveness of safeguards.

[3]As detailed in the Remelink Report; see endnote one of chapter nine.

Chapter 15

[1]For further reading on the argument for personal autonomy, and the critique of it, refer to endnote one of chapter six.

[2]Hendin argues that rather than increasing patient autonomy, legalizing PAS will actually undermine it: "The Dutch experience indicates that legalization has undermined patient autonomy because ultimately it is the doctor, and not the patient, who determines the choice for death; the patient is often deprived of the power to choose." He goes on to say that "legal acceptance has encouraged physicians to feel they are best able to make the decision as to who should live and who should die" (*Seduced by Death,* 1st ed., pp. 179, 183).

Chapter 16

[1]This is Ogden's point referred to in endnote one of chapter seven. See also Chamberlain, "Physician Assisted Suicide," pp. 3-4 for a brief critique of Ogden's position.

[2]These differences were spelled out at the previously mentioned forums with Faye Girsh.

Chapter 17

[1]This argument was made by Mark Pickup, a disabled man, in a speech given at the University of Saskatchewan in October 1997.

[2]For further research showing that disabled people rate their own quality of life virtually identically to the way able-bodied people rate theirs, see K. A. Gerhart et al., "Quality of Life Following Spinal Cord Injury: Knowledge and Attitudes of Emergency Care Workers," *Annals of Emergency Medicine* 23 (1994): 807-12; P. Cameron et al., "The Life Satisfaction of Nonnormal Persons." *Journal of Consulting and Clinical Psychology* 41 (1973): 207-14; C. Ray and J. West, "Social, Sexual and Personal Implications of Paraplegia," *Paraplegia* 22 (1984): 75-86; and M. G. Eisenberg and C. C. Saltz, "Quality of Life Among Aging Spinal Cord Injured Persons: Long Term Rehabilitation Outcomes," *Paraplegia* 29 (1991): 514-20.

Chapter 19

[1]This is an actual survey conducted by TTI Market Explorers in Vancouver, British Columbia, in 1997. In the survey 603 people throughout the province were questioned. The poll has a margin of error of plus or minus 4 percent, nineteen times out of twenty.